A Coup' of Sorts

A Coup' of Sorts

A Novella

By

Howard S. Rosenzweig, Ph.D.

Disclaimer:
This book is a work of fiction. Names, characters, places, and events are either products of the author's imagination or are used fictitiously. Any resemblance to actual events, locales, or persons [other than historical individuals], living or dead, is entirely coincidental.

© 2012 Howard Rosenzweig
All rights reserved.

Dedication and Acknowledgement

I firmly believe that no man (or woman) is an island. In order to succeed in life, one must accept the help and support of others. I have truly been blessed for both the family and friends I have had in my life.

Without the love and support of my precious wife Maria and equally precious son Vasilios, I could not have found the time to write this novella. Without these two wonderful people, my life would be truly lonesome and without purpose. Whatever success I have, it is done for them as well.

Without the love and support of my dear mother Pearl and of my beloved late father Carl, I wouldn't have grown up to become the human being, scientist and songwriter I sought to be. My brother Les would always protect me, and to me is as an example of a truly brave man.

The love of my beloved mother-in-law Kally, my beloved late father-in-law Vasilios and my caring and loving sister-in-law Litsa is another pillar of support in my life.

To all the many caring family members and friends I have not named, know that you are in my heart and mind; for those of you who have fallen out of favor with me, know that you are somewhere else!

And without the help many years ago of my friend Robert Allison, I doubt if this story would have the ring of truth I hope it possesses.

Chapter 1

North Vietnam, 1970

It is morning as Vietnamese boys and girls are playing tag in front of a French Style colonial mansion. Their laughter and giggles fill the air. Armed soldiers walk along the perimeter. One of them takes a drag on a cigarette, then glances back to the mansion, where the children are now crowding around the living room window. They're making faces to someone inside, as a General is running comically to the window from the inside, shooing them away. As the children scurry off, one of them stays behind, and watches as the Vietcong General walks back to a large, rectangular table surrounded by a group of officers. The General points to several locations in South Vietnam on a map on a bulletin board, as the officers nod in agreement.

After night falls, in an upstairs bedroom of the Vietcong General's mansion, a beautiful Vietnamese woman is lying in a luxurious king size bed, as she lifts up the blanket to reveal her slender, naked body. The VC General looks back to her, a big smile on his face as he gets out of his chair by his work desk and walks to the window. He grabs the curtains on both sides of the window as the crack of a rifle is followed by the General being shot through his forehead. The General is knocked down, as blood pumps out of the back of his head onto the wooden floor.

Up in a banyon tree, two thousand yards away, an American soldier-assassin, hair shoulder length, is still aiming his sniper rifle towards the mansion.

The naked woman bursts through the front door, screaming and crying as she runs towards the courtyard where the children played earlier that day. Her husband's blood is on her hands and breasts.

The American assassin, Les Cohen, has a look of sadness and regret on his face, as he points his gun at the woman. The woman's face is seen in his rifle scope's cross hairs, when suddenly a North Vietnamese officer grabs her by the shoulders in front of her, his back to Cohen. He shakes her, trying to calm her down, when he suddenly falls on top of her and drops them both to the ground, after he's shot in the back. She struggles to push him off of her, and finally starts to get up from the ground.

The woman's head again is in his rifle scope's cross hairs, as she looks around silently in shock. Cohen starts to pull the trigger, then stops himself suddenly. "Forget it." mumbling to himself. Cohen shoulders his rifle as he quickly climbs down the tree. He starts to run towards the dense forest as he hears the shouts of other VC searching for him.

South America, 1385

Gentle sunlight graces the Mayan city in all its splendor. The city is dominated by its central, pyramid temple. The marketplace is already filling, as the sounds of the many craftsmen and produce sellers bark their wares.

From the top of the pyramid the sun is seen on the horizon, as birds fly across its face. The temple draws closer to us, as its entrance on the top of the pyramid is reached, we start to enter it.

Deep within the temple, a young man is lying naked in a large bed, with two young, attractive, slender, naked women lying next to him, one on each side. One of the women starts to kiss him on the mouth, as he starts to awaken. The other women gets up and unlocks a cabinet and removes a goblet from it. She comes back into the bed and sits beside the man. She pours some of the red liquid on the nipples of her breasts, as he starts to suckle them greedily. She then gives him the goblet to drink from, as the other woman gets out of the bed, puts a robe on and then leaves the room.

The other woman starts to massage the man's neck from behind, and then suddenly a look of fear touches her face, as three priests walk into the room. She gets up silently and leaves quickly, without bothering to cover herself.

The young man has a dazed look on his face, as two of the priests help him out of the bed. They hold him gently by the arms as they lead him out of the room, followed by the third priest. They walk down a brightly lit spiral staircase, the walls covered with brightly colored pictures of Mayan life. They reach a central chamber sealed by a large wooden door. One of two guards standing beside it pulls it open. The two priests continue to assist the young man inside, and as the third priest passes by the guards, they seal the door behind him.

The chamber is brightly lit, from both many oil lamps, as well as a beam of sunlight reflected down a shaft by a mirror near the top of the temple. The beam of sunlight bathes down directly onto a stone oval platform in the center of the chamber. The two priests bring the young man next to the oval platform, where one can see fresh blood radiating out from its center. They help the young man to lie on his back, as they start to gently chant.

They place slip knots around his wrists as they tie the ropes to poles sticking out the sides of the oval. They continue to chant as they fasten down his feet in a similar fashion.

The young man starts to come to, as he realizes he can't move. He looks around to see the circular wall of the chamber come into focus. The circular wall of the chamber depicts a man in various stages of being placed down on a similar oval platform, the second scene showing him being tied down.

As his eyes pan across the circular wall, the third scene depicts his hands and feet being held down by two priests. With mounting fear on his face, the young man scans the rest of this macabre zoetrope. The next scene shows the third priest stabbing the man through his chest, followed by pulling his bloody heart out of his chest.

The young man starts to pull frantically on his ropes as the two priests press his arms and legs down. He looks up to see the third priest's stone cold face, as he lifts up a knife in both hands and then plunges it down.....

South America, January 24th, 1979

A hatchet cuts off a chicken's head. A burly man hands the still shaking chicken from the neck to his wife, as he joins other men leaving the village.

They walk towards a clearing in the jungle......

A large crowd is gathered in a jungle clearing near the village of Jualape, in the South American nation of San Mateo. At the front of the audience, standing on a table serving as a stand, is a tall, thin, mid-forties Catholic priest named Father Lupe. There is a large din from the crowd, who are all standing, until he starts to speak, upon which they become silent.

"People of Jualape; my dear friends and family, I stand here before you a failed man. Five years ago, we had supported The General in his successful toppling of the evil Carlos Mendoza. As so often happens in history, our old dictatorship was replaced by another, more heinous one. His right hand man, Rodriguez, who heads the Muertemos, has been responsible for the torture and murder of thousands of our people. I tried to follow the teachings of Jesus; I've tried to use the techniques of Gandhi to bring a peaceful resolution to our plight and have failed you all. The United Nations has abandoned us, as they have abandoned the Palestinians and the Kurds. The world turns away as the number of our "Disappeared Ones" increases with each passing year. The U.S. government continues to support The General, for he provides them with a desired military base, cheap labor for the American companies here as well as being staunchly anti-communist. But now is the time for all this to change! Before I leave this Earth, and I fear it will be very soon, I will call upon whatever power is necessary to end our despair."

The crowd becomes very agitated. Looks of worry are on their faces. A man near the front, an unkempt, unshaven man in his late fifties named Dr. Aramos, claps at what Father Lupe has just said. Father Lupe smiles back at him. Aramos looks back to him with sorrowful, empty eyes.

At an adjacent edge of the jungle clearing, a man dressed in camouflage is seen clicking photographs. In the camera's lens, it is Dr. Aramos's picture that is being taken.

The rest of the crowd starts to clap, when one of the men calls out, "How will you do that Father Lupe?"

"I can not tell you that, for I don't want the evil that I will set forth to hurt any of the innocent."

"Whatever you do we shall face it together Padre."

The priest is moved by this. "I will let myself be martyred for our cause, but not before I place a curse upon everyone involved with my demise. I shall call upon a lackey of the Devil himself to seek our revenge!"

The crowd shows a mixture of shock and disbelief. A number of those present cross themselves.

"Now, please, go back to your homes. I don't have much time before they come for me." The village slowly disperses, while Dr. Aramos stays behind. After the clearing has emptied, he joins Father Lupe as they walk toward the dense rain forest to the North.

The same man hidden at the clearing's edge clicks photographs of Dr. Aramos and Father Lupe together as they walk to the end of the clearing. Dr. Aramos and Father Lupe are seen through the lens of the camera. The camera clicks their image several times before they slip away into the Northern Jungle.

Warsaw Ghetto, April 1943

The rifle's scope of the Waffen SS sniper sweeps across a squalid street in the ghetto. It starts to track a teenage girl and a five year old boy walking next to her. The gun scope's cross hairs switch back and forth between the girl and boy, focusing on the yellow Star of David on the chest of their jackets. The children stop for a moment, to pick something up off the street. They stand up again and start to walk.

A yellow Star of David nearly fills the gun sight's view, with its cross hairs bouncing up and down within the Jewish Star's shape. The crack of the rifle's shot pierces the silence, as the little boy is shot through the heart. He flies down onto his back, as the girl falls to the ground to embrace him. She cries out in anguish as she rocks the dead boy in her arms.

Her head is now seen in the cross hairs of the gun sight as she is suddenly pulled out of its point of view. The sniper now has a look of frustration on his face, as he sees a door of the building the children were next to slam shut.

Inside that building, a man is trying to calm the girl down, holding her close to him as she cries and screams.

Upstairs, we see twin brothers, their faces bathed in firelight, as they look at each other as they hear the girl's screams from downstairs. The boys are lying down on the floor of an upstairs apartment, looking down through a large opening into an adjacent apartment diagonally below them.

They see the back of a man wrapped in a prayer shawl, as he prays before a man lying down on a mattress on the floor. The young man on the mattress is writhing in pain. The twins' gaze are transfixed on the ceremony.

The young man suddenly stops his cries of torment and just lies motionless on the mattress.

The Rabbi now faces us, as he kneels down to the motionless young man. Above the Rabbi's head, the twins are seen looking down at them. "Will he be alright Papa?" questions Judah.

"You shouldn't be here boys. You're too young to witness this ritual," Rabbi Gershon answers.

"Papa, I don't think God cares one way or the other," Saul answers sarcastically.

"Bite your tongue Saul. Come down to help me with Joshua." The boys hurry down..........

The door that the teenage girl was pulled to safety through suddenly bursts open, as the young man named Joshua walks out with no fear. Anger fills his mind as he sees the dead boy on the ground. He scans the street in the direction from which the sniper fired from. From a building across the street he sees the momentary glint of sunlight reflecting from the rifle's scope.

The Waffen SS sniper lines up his target. In his gun's scope, he sees the young man smiling at him. The sniper pauses for a moment. His brief look of puzzlement changes to an arrogant smirk. The sniper shoots him in the head, as the young man falls to the ground. The sniper scans the area with his scope. A look of surprise comes to his face, when he notices the young man's body is gone where he had fallen just moments ago. He puts his rifle down for a moment, when he suddenly notices a figure dashing inhumanly fast to the side of his building on his right. He wipes his eyes and shakes his head. He resumes looking through his rifle's scope, but then suddenly stops when he hears creaking on the hallway's floor. He turns around to face the doorway, fear on his face. He gets up and moves tiptoe to the gutted room's doorway. The sniper peers out into the hallway, as he points his rifle from elbow level. He cranes his neck forward to try to hear better. As the sniper concentrates his gaze out into the hallway, Joshua lowers himself silently down with one arm holding a beam, right behind him. The sniper's look of fear turns to shock the moment his neck is broken by the young man, as Joshua twists his head 180 degrees around. The sniper's limp body crumbles down, as the young man picks up the rifle and ammo, and walks out the doorway.....

South America, San Mateo-January 24th, 1979

Soon after Father Lupe and Dr. Aramos leave the clearing, they find two knapsacks hidden for them. As they walk, the jungle becomes more dense. The sunlight is becoming more diffuse due to the rain forest's thickening canopy. As they trek, it is clear that Aramos is getting exhausted. His face is haggard. He stops to catch his breath. They lean against a tree and drink water from canteens, wiping the sweat from their brows. Aramos leans with his back and slides down the trunk of the tree to sit on the ground. He lets out a sigh.
"I'm not as young as I used to be. Forgive me Juan for slowing you down."
"Don't speak nonsense Hector. We will be there shortly. Do you think the Americano will be happy with my speech?"
"I believe so. It seemed to have the right effect on the village. What I am unhappy about is the great risk you're willing to take in trusting him; to allow him to arrange for your 'assassination.'"
"Hector, the risk I take is far less than what you are about to do. You are my brother, the only real family I have. There is great danger in what you're about to undertake."
"After my Luisa was murdered, I have lost nearly every desire to live. Only the chance to achieve revenge, to make our revolution succeed, helps me to go on."

Father Lupe places his arm around Aramos's shoulder, sadness apparent on his face. Father Lupe gets up and offers his right hand to Aramos, who grabs it and lets Lupe help him up.

"Come, let's walk." Lupe and Aramos start to walk towards a small hill in the distance.

"Anyway Hector, the Americano is a man of honor. You saw with your own eyes how bravely he fought to overthrow Mendoza."

"Yes, that's true. But he is also a mercenary. How can you be so sure he will not betray us?"

"One can never be sure of that, but because of what Ariana has confided in me, I believe he is sincere in wanting to help us. And remember, most organizations, be they governments or crime families, are normally destroyed from the inside."

"I hope you are right. However, we wouldn't be here if we trusted him completely."

"Let's just say that God helps those who help themselves." The men came upon a small hill, whose peak still remained below the rain forest's canopy. At the top of the hill, four trees were growing close to each other, obscuring what appeared to be some sort of dwelling. As they reach the top, a door of loose vines and leaves is slightly ajar.

"It appears our friend is already here," as Father Lupe points towards the entrance.

"Was he surprised about where the ritual would take place?"

"Of course. This Mayan Temple is one of the great, "undiscovered" archaeological finds in the world."

"He wasn't disturbed by the choice of location?"

"No, he agreed that secrecy was paramount, and that he could adapt the ceremonial chamber to our needs."

"Well then, let's go join him. I'm anxious to meet him at last."

The men go in after lighting two torches with a cigarette lighter. They slowly wind down the internal passageways, Mayan hieroglyphics as well as frightening pagan sculptures coming into view and disappearing as their torches pass them by. They carefully walk down a spiral staircase. They finally come upon a central chamber, whose ancient wooden door is slightly ajar, the beam of light from inside welcoming them in. As they open the door, the bright light from many torches temporarily blinds them. As their eyes adjust, they see that the circular wall is covered with white bed sheets. Near the center on top of a folding table is a small tabernacle with a large Star of David on top of it. The tabernacle doors have the Ten Commandments decorating them, enclosing a Torah inside. The table also has a lit candelabrum on it, along with an ancient manuscript and a goblet with red liquid in it.

At the very center is a stone oval platform about 3 feet high, also covered with white bed sheets.

"Rabbi Avenidas!"

"Father Lupe, my dear friend!" They embrace each other warmly. As the Rabbi approaches Aramos, Aramos is unconsciously taken aback by the disfigured left eye of Avenidas.

"Forgive me Dr. Aramos. Normally I would wear an eye patch, but the ceremony calls for not hiding any deformity."

"No, I wish to be forgiven Rabbi. I feel ashamed. I was once a medical doctor, a surgeon in fact. I thought I was immune to such things."

"Please, there's no need to explain. I am so sorry about your daughter. I only hope that what we do today will give you some peace."

"If you are successful Rabbi, I will be in your debt."

Rabbi Avenidas starts to wrap phylacteries around his right arm and then finishes with one on his forehead. His head is covered by a yarmulke. Aramos notices the large number tattooed on Avenidas's left fore arm.

"Rabbi, if you don't mind me asking, where did you get that?"

"Auschwitz."

"I am so very sorry. Perhaps it is you who should undergo the transformation, for you obviously have suffered much more in your life."

"Perhaps, but I have had over thirty years to come to terms with what had happened to my family and I. I now have a loving wife and children. I have my community's respect as their Rabbi. However, that doesn't mean that I have found true peace by any means. For this ritual, we need a person whose loss and pain has left them hollow, and the more recent the horror that befell them has occurred, the more likely it will succeed."

"I can't imagine ever feeling whole again after what the Muertemos did to my only child, my only daughter." Aramos seems ready to cry, then stops himself.

"I know how you feel. Did Juan explain to you what we are about to do?"

"He told me that you would use Kaballa to transform me into an agent of God. Why do you need a "hollow" man?"

"Are you familiar with the legend of the Golem?"

"A little."

"The Golem was created out of inanimate material in the shape of a giant man and brought to life through the Rabbi of Prague's use of Kabbala sorcery. Its history is actually much more ancient. As with most legends, the Golem is based on truth as well. Throughout the millennia, most Rabbis skilled in this mystic practice feared to enact the ritual. It was eventually learned that a living human male could be substituted for the effigy. The person transformed retained his memory of his past life and was bound as an agent of God to be righteous in meting out justice."

"Isn't there too much temptation for such a person to act out his own design for revenge, and therefore possibly kill the innocent?" Father Lupe asked.

"Yes there is. That's why the Rabbi who created the Golem had to be prepared to destroy him as well."

"What if the Golem murders the Rabbi before he could stop him?" questions Dr. Aramos.

"If that would happen, the Golem would be consumed to dust, for he could not exist if the Rabbi dies. I guess you could call it God's failsafe mechanism………

Warsaw Ghetto, April 1943

Three SS run for cover and jump into a nearby bomb crater in the street, as gun shots are heard.

"I can't believe that Jews have guns!" shouted the SS corporal.

An SS lieutenant sitting next to him nods in agreement. An SS sergeant sits on the opposite end of the crater.

"What could be worse than a Jew with a gun?" asks the SS Sergeant.

"Me!" As the young man named Joshua kneels over the crater's edge, he grabs the SS Corporal and SS Lieutenant by their heads and smashes them together. Their helmets crack open as they lean against each other like rag dolls. Joshua jumps into the crater and lands solidly on his feet, as he slowly walks towards the SS Sergeant. The SS Sergeant pulls out his Luger and starts to shoot Joshua in the chest. Joshua keeps moving forward, and as he laughs he reveals sharp fangs. A look of horror is now on the SS Sergeant's face, as his Luger is empty and Joshua keeps walking closer to him......

Moments earlier, in the ghetto building where Joshua was transformed into a Golem, a Waffen SS Captain is inside a 1st floor apartment, as he listens carefully as he walks slowly across the floor. He carries a flame thrower. Suddenly he stops, as he notices a loud creaking sound. He removes a carpet and quickly opens the hideaway's entrance. He points the flame thrower into the secret basement.

"Raus Juden!"

Rabbi Gershon moves into view, followed by his twin sons. "We will come peacefully." The three of them climb out, one by one, using a chair as a step ladder. They walk out of the room with their hands above their heads. The Rabbi and his sons walk ahead of the Waffen SS Captain down a hallway and into the foyer. They all walk out into the street. The Waffen SS Captain stops the children on the sidewalk, as he lets the Rabbi walk ahead onto the road. The Waffen SS Captain motions with his hand for an SS Private to hold the children. The SS Private stands behind the twins, holding them by the scruffs of their necks.

"I bet your father is part of the rebellion." Judah and Saul look pleadingly at the Waffen SS Captain. (To the Rabbi) "Isn't that right you Jew bastard?" The Waffen SS starts to point his flame thrower at the Rabbi's sons. The SS Private suddenly looks very uncomfortable.

"Please, don't hurt my boys. Yes, I'm the leader. They're not responsible for my actions. Take me, I won't resist."

"That won't be necessary." The Waffen SS fires his flame thrower, the arc of its long flame reaches the Rabbi in the street, as his whole body is engulfed in flames.

"Nooooooooooooooooooo!" Judah and Saul cry out……..

Back in the bomb crater, Joshua is starting to bite the SS Sergeant in the neck, as he suddenly turns to dust and crumbles away. The SS Sergeant touches his neck with his shaking right hand, and is relieved to see only a little blood on his palm. "Danke Gott in himmel!" The broad smile on his face disappears as a bullet pierces his throat.

A middle aged Jewish man is looking through the sniper rifle's scope, from the roof of a nearby building, a broad smile now on his face……….

San Mateo-11:53 AM, January 24th, 1979

Back in the Mayan sacrificial chamber, Rabbi Avenidas has a far away look on his face. He wipes a tear from his eye. "Forgive me. Where was I? Oh yes. As I said, the Golem would turn to dust upon the death of the Rabbi who created him. This can be viewed as both a blessing and a curse. I am a young man Dr. Aramos. However, once I transform you, your life will be literally in my hands. If you become derelict in your duties, I would be forced to destroy you. If the Muertemos get their hands on me and kill me, you would die as well. Are you willing to take that chance?"

"I wouldn't be here otherwise. My brother swears that you are a man of honor and from seeing you myself I believe it is so." Aramos pauses for a moment. "You mentioned before that the chosen man had to be hollow from his grief, in order for the ritual to work."

"Yes, that is quite so. If the person has not been so "prepared" by such horror and pain, so they can act as a receptacle, if you will, for a fraction of God's power to enter him, then he will surely die."

"I presume that was learned by trial and error." Father Lupe asked.

"You are correct my friend. Even for the ones that the ritual is successful, the transformation is extremely painful. You need to remember that the ritual was originally designed to bring inanimate clay to life as the Golem."

"Why would any Rabbi think that using a living person would be an improvement over clay?"

"I believe that the person's very humanity would allow the Rabbi to reason with the Human Golem if he turned against the community's interest. The Human Golem retains the memory of their past life, and this tie to humanity also helps to keep him focused on God's chosen path."

"So, is the Human Golem alive? Or does the transformation cause the person to die, only to be replaced by an empty shell, a soulless ghost?" Father Lupe shows concern in his eyes.

"My friend, the Human Golem, as far as I know, is still alive, is still capable of love and empathy, but he is nonetheless changed."

Dr. Aramos is standing near the goblet now, and as he points to the red liquid within it he says: "Must I drink blood for its success?"

"No, that will come later." Both Father Lupe and Dr. Aramos show fear for the first time. "The goblet has no blood. It is datura tea diluted with red wine. It is a highly effective anesthetic. In fact, ironically, it was used in temples just like this one to keep the human sacrifice placid before their still beating heart was ripped from their chest."

"Tell me Judah, why didn't your people create Golems during the Holocaust? If ever there was a time to use them, one would expect them to be used against the Nazis and their collaborators."

"They did Juan. They did it in places like the Treblinka Death Camp, as well as in the Warsaw Ghetto. But as I said before, if the Rabbi who performed the ritual was murdered, the Human Golem perished with him. My brother and I witnessed our own Father create a Golem in Warsaw, but my Father was murdered before our very eyes during the ghetto uprising and so his Human Golem could not help the resistance long enough." Avenidas pauses, as a look of sadness mixed with guilt washes over his face. "Presumably the same thing happened in Treblinka. However, due to the brave fighters' planning and courage, four hundred people did escape from that death camp, to bear witness to the horrors committed there, though it is believed only around forty ultimately survived." Avenidas pauses, his head down as if in prayer. He suddenly looks up with optimism on his face. "Anyway my friends, are you ready?"

"Yes we are." Aramos and Lupe reply in unison.

"Good! Dr. Aramos, if you would be so kind to remove your clothes and put on this robe." Dr. Aramos took the plain white cotton robe and placed it temporarily on the sacrificial altar. He quickly disrobed and placed his clothes off to the side of the room. He put the robe on from over his head, finding it reached down nearly to the floor. Rabbi Avenidas placed his tallis over his head.

"Please sit down for a moment," as Rabbi Avenidas points at the sacrificial altar. Aramos slowly sits down on its edge close to Avenidas. Rabbi Avenidas grabs the goblet with both hands and holding it above his head, starts to recite a blessing as he faces the tabernacle holding the Torah inside. "Blessed is the Lord, King of the Universe, who provides us with this balm to ease the pain of thy ritual." Avenidas gently hands the goblet to Aramos. "It's best to drink this in one gulp, otherwise you might throw up from it." Aramos takes a brief smell of it and winces. He then gulps most of it down before he starts to cough. Avenidas gently slaps him on the back, and by the time when his cough has calmed, Aramos already has a distant look on his face. "The datura tea is already effecting him Juan."

"I noticed. Let's hope it will protect him long enough."

"I believe it will. Your brother Hector is a brave, strong man. I believe he'll be alright. Please, help me to lay him down on the altar." Lupe and Avenidas gently move Aramos, helping him to lie down on his back on the sacrificial altar. Avenidas hands a yarmulke to Lupe. Lupe puts it on his head.

"Once I start the ritual, you must not stop me as I transform your brother. He may scream in anguish, I warn you. Do you wish to leave my friend?"

"No Judah, I must stay by Hector, even if I end up having to offer him the last rites," Lupe's eyes show his concern and fear.

Avenidas goes over to the folding table and opens the old manuscript towards the last third of the book. He reads from it to himself for a short time, then places it back on the table, open where he had read from. He covers his eyes with his right hand and starts to quietly pray to himself, rhythmically bowing up and down in front of the tabernacle containing the Torah. He soon turns to face Dr. Aramos, who stares away into the distance, seemingly unaware of what is happening around him. Avenidas raises his hands above his head, palms outward, forming a symbolic Hebrew letter shin from the two "v"'s obtained, one from each hand[1]. He closes his eyes and begins:

"Dear Lord, King of the Universe, we call upon your Eternal Spirit to enter the man before you. He has been made hollow by the wickedness of the world, and wishes to be made into your instrument for justice." Suddenly a chill fills the room, as a wind seemingly from nowhere passes through, extinguishing nearly all of the torches within. The room is dark now except for the light around the altar. Aramos begins to move and moan from pain.

"King of the Universe, place your mighty hand upon him, give him the strength of twenty men, give him the vision of a falcon and the wisdom to mete out justice as an agent in your service." Aramos starts to scream and convulse as if he were epileptic, his hands strangely held behind his back. Lupe starts to move towards him, then suddenly stops himself, remembering the Rabbi's warning.

In his state of transformation, Dr. Aramos finds himself back in his home's living room, about to relive the horror that befell his daughter and him just five months ago…

His hands are tied behind his back as he's forced to sit on a recliner. A Muertemos is pointing a gun to his head as he is forced to watch his daughter Luisa being raped by two other Muertemos. She is spread-eagled at the edge of the coach, as the 2nd Muertemos forcefully engages intercourse A third one holds a knife to her throat. The 2nd one starts to move back and forth very quickly, as Luisa cries out in pain.

"Stop it! Stop it! We've done nothing wrong. Kill me if you want but stop raping my daughter," Dr. Aramos pleads. Tears are streaming down his face.

"We'll do whatever we want old man," the 1st Muertemos replies. "We'll fuck your putana daughter till she's raw inside if we want, since there's nothing you can do about it." The Muertemos

---

[1] This is the same hand gesture made famous by Leonard Nimoy for the Vulcan hand salute in Star Trek.

starts to slap Aramos with the back of his hand. Suddenly the 2nd Muertemos starts to moan as he comes inside Luisa. He pulls out of her and pulls up his pants.

"I'm finished. Let's get the hell out of here," the 2nd Muertemos orders. The 3rd Muertemos starts to slit Luisa's throat.

"Noooooooooooooooooooooooooooooo!"

Father Lupe doesn't understand why his brother is screaming. He feels helpless as he continues to watch and listen to the ritual.

"Let him live to serve you, to be a light upon the evil that surrounds us, to be your sword to crush those who do not live by your commandments." Aramos arches his back and screams horribly. Lupe is at his wits end.

"Give him this purpose, give him this power so thy people will be freed from the evil ones." Aramos screams one last time and collapses. A wind once more passes through the room, and as it leaves the extinguished torches are relit, bathing the room in a warm, gentle light. Father Lupe and Rabbi Avenidas look down upon Aramos, who is silent and unmoving. Lupe looks towards Avenidas, who indicates for him to go to his brother. Lupe embraces his brother, crying.

"I never should have let him do this."

"I'm so sorry Juan. I thought he would make it."

As Father Lupe raises his right hand and makes the sign of the cross, he speaks through his tears: "In nomine Patris, et Filii, et Spiritus Sancti, ego te absolvo a peccatis tuis." Lupe and Avenidas face away from Aramos. They cry together. They suddenly jump forward together as well, apparently goosed from behind.

"What the hell are you doing? I'm not dead yet Juan."

"Hector, you're alive! We thought the ritual was too much for you." Avenidas is beaming, joy openly expressed on his face as he joins Lupe in helping Aramos get up.

Chapter 2

The next day, in the Arroyo neighborhood of San Tomas, two Muertemos are banging on Dr. Aramos's front door at 5 AM. The door flies open. Aramos has a wild look on his face, as the two men are taken aback.

"You must come with us Dr. Aramos," orders the 1st Muertemos.

Aramos has a smirk on his face. He starts to close his door.

"What the fuck? If you don't want anything bad to happen to Father Lupe," (a look of concern, then anger on Aramos's face) then you better come right now."

Aramos is led to a black van with no windows. He steps inside as the back doors are locked behind him. Aramos settles himself on the bench as the van pulls away. As he closes his eyes, he starts to see an old memory:

A little girl is lying in bed, covered with a blanket up to her neck. Her eyes are open, and a look of joy comes to her face as she looks to her door and sees a young man enter.

"Daddy! You're finally home!" Luisa runs out of the bed to hug her father. He gets on his knees to embrace her and kiss her warmly. He stands up and picks her up in his arms. He brings her gently back to the bed.

"How are you my Dulcinita? I missed you so much!"

"I missed you too Padre! What made you late tonight?"

"A young boy had fallen down on his head. I had to perform an emergency operation."

"Is he alright?"

"Yes my darling. Now you go to sleep, for tomorrow we have a big day in store for us."

"Then it's true? Mommy said we're going to the zoo," a look of excitement fills Luisa's pretty face.

"That's right, I need to see some of my relatives!"

"Oh Daddy, stop joking around." Luisa starts to yawn, as Dr. Aramos covers her up to her neck and kisses her on her forehead.

"Good night my Luisa," Aramos gently whispers.

A pothole jars Aramos from his reverie, as tears are welling in his eyes, as the van rocks back and forth.

Muertemos Interrogation Center - 5:40 AM, January 25th, 1979

As Les Cohen walks down the basement corridor, the guards of the Muertemos snap to attention. Sobs of pain can be heard behind the bolted metal doors as he passes them by. As he reaches the end of the hallway, he stares at the guard through his mirrored sunglasses, who immediately opens the door. The interrogation cell has a metal chair bolted to the floor in the room's center. Dr. Aramos is strapped down to it. A sturdy wooden table stands nearby, upon which is seated Colonel Rodriquez, who is toying with surgical instruments that are spread along the table. Along each of the three walls facing the open door is placed a gurney covered with a large white bed sheet, apparently concealing a body underneath. As Rodriquez observes how light reflecting off a scalpel in his hand plays upon Dr. Aramos's face, he doesn't notice how Aramos is starting to break the straps holding his hands down. At this moment Cohen walks in. The guard quickly closes the door behind him.

"What are you doing here Sanchez?", as Cohen moves next to Aramos.

"I'm simply applying some incentive for our guest."

"The last three times you've applied your correspondence course surgical skills, we ended up with no further leads dealing with the resistance."

"Call me, irresponsible. Here, what do you think of this?" Rodriguez hands Cohen photographs showing Aramos with Father Lupe at the jungle clearing near the village of Jualape. Cohen looks briefly at them, then quickly hands them back.

"Isn't this clear evidence that he is a key person in Father Lupe's resistance movement?," a look of triumph on Rodriguez's face.

"He is definitely a key person to Lupe, but some simple inquiries would have let you realize that they are simply brothers, not conspirators." Rodriguez looks embarrassed and pissed off.

"Why don't you make yourself useful somewhere else Sanchez, while I talk to the good doctor about how he might help us."

"I am no traitor to my people."

"You see, what did I tell you?," as a smirk returns to Rodriguez's face.

"You saw his file Colonel. Any self respecting man would never chose to help us after what your Muertemos did. Now go."

"Alright, I need to meet with another "client". He going to be "shocked" if you catch my drift."

"Why don't you just try some sodium pentathol instead?"

"And miss all the fun?," a look of feigned shock on his face. Rodriguez walks over and bangs on the cell door. The guard quickly opens it. As he leaves, he turns to the guard and orders: "No one else is to enter this cell until I say otherwise."

"I understand Colonel." The guard quickly closes the door, leaving Cohen and Aramos 'alone'."

"Dr. Aramos, I apologize for this indignity." The doctor looks suspiciously at the American, then at the surgical instruments.

"Don't worry Doctor Aramos, these instruments were never meant for you, despite what Rodriguez may have told you." Cohen proceeds to unstrap the doctor, surprised that the hand restraints are nearly severed from the chair's arms.

"Why did you have me brought here? I already have helped you to get my brother's cooperation."

"First, to thank you and also ask for your help in a delicate matter."

"And if I refuse?"

"Then I'll have to arrange to have your brother's "assassination" to be no fraud." The anger wells up in Aramos, and he's ready to strike at Cohen. "But I have no desire to hurt you or your brother. I chose your brother not only because he's a charismatic leader, but also because of you." Aramos calms himself, surprised by what Cohen said "You possess the medical skills I require." Cohen walks over very close to him. "See that peristaltic pump over there?"

Aramos nods affirmatively.

"I want you to take this steel sculpture, and...," in Cohen's hand one can see it's a set of the upper human teeth, however with unusually long canines. Cohen leans down and starts to whisper to him in his left ear, his back to our view. Aramos's eyes start to look menacing, as he starts to open his mouth, revealing unusually large canines of his own. He begins to turn his head close to Cohen's neck; he's ready to bite him, however, he suddenly has a look of surprise on his face, followed by incredulity. His canines diminish back to normal size.

"You must be mad. I may be a washed up surgeon, but I still obey the Hippocratic Oath."

"That's very noble of you Aramos. I realize this is a very difficult thing I must ask of you. I know deep down that you're anything but washed up. Your file indicates that..." All of a sudden the lights flicker on and off for several seconds. Inside the peristaltic pump, its fuse has blown.

Outside the Interrogation Center, lightning is seen striking the building.

"That imbecile Rodriguez, when will he ever learn? Forgive me Dr. Aramos, your file indicates that your daughter was raped and murdered before your eyes by three members of the Muertemos. Your renowned medical career ended after that. I believe a man of your stature should not lose anymore then you already have. The best way to prevent the loss of your expertise is to practice. I also believe that when one is called upon to do something unpleasant, in order to make it bearable, one should couple it to something pleasurable." Cohen begins walking around the room, uncovering each gurney as he passes them by. Strapped down on each of the movable tables lies a man stripped down to only his underwear, their mouths gagged. Aramos's eyes brighten and then show amazement followed by malice. Cohen notices his reaction and is pleased.

"I gather by your expression that these are the pieces of shit that raped and murdered your daughter Luisa."

"Yes."

"Well doctor, I will leave you now to practice. I hope I didn't forget any instruments you might need. However, we unfortunately have no anesthetic, though I'm sure you'll have their best interest in heart." The doctor just nodded.

"When you feel that you've practiced enough, please then proceed with the chore that I requested. Is that amenable to you?"

"Yes, yes it is. Why are you doing this?"

"As I said before, I wanted to thank you for your help, as well as to aid in your regaining your surgical skills. When you are finished, the guard will escort you to get shaved and showered, and then you will be brought to me." Cohen bangs the door. The guard quickly opens it. As he leaves, he turns to see Dr. Aramos with his three "patients", their eyes bulging out as they watch Aramos open and close a pair of huge scissors. The guard quickly closes the door after Cohen leaves. Cohen walks briskly down the opposite way along the same hallway that he used to get to the interrogation cell. The guards once again snap to attention.

Aramos proceeds to viciously rip off the tape gagging the Muertemos' mouths, one after the other. "Please feel free to scream." Aramos approaches one of the Muertemos with the huge pair of scissors. The Muertemos standing guard outside the cell winces as he hears the screams from inside.

Cohen walks out of the Muertemos Interrogation Center. The thunderstorm already has passed through. Cohen breathes with relish the fresh air. Henry notices him and drives the limo up front to pick him up. Cohen opens the back door himself and gets in.

"Did you hear that lightning hit the building sir?"

A look of surprise is on Cohen's face. "No, you can't hear shit in that dungeon. I thought it was Rodriguez who caused the power trouble."

"I'd prefer to blame it on Rodriguez sir.

"Me too, but we'll have to the let the prick off easy this time.," as both Cohen and Henry smile. He begins to quietly read a newspaper as he is driven through the center of the capitol. The streets are bustling with people window shopping. Some vendors on the sidewalks are selling fresh fruit and nuts, while other sell fresh bread. Near a street corner, a kiosk is selling cigarettes, newspapers and magazines. Cohen is still quietly reading his newspaper as the limo reaches the Presidential Palace. The limo stops by the guard at the gate, who upon seeing Cohen in the back seat immediately has the gate opened for the limo to drive through. The limo drives up to the Palace's front, and Cohen gets out and takes several wrapped packages and two long, narrow boxes from the trunk. He nods to Henry before he pulls the limo away. As Cohen walks up the front entrance, the two attending guards snap to attention and salute, as Cohen bows his head in turn.

Moments later, Cohen is ringing the doorbell of an upstairs suite. The door opens and ones sees a mature, lovely woman.

"Les! How are you? Please come in."

"You are lovely as ever Esmerelda. These are for you." Cohen hands her one of the long, narrow boxes sealed with a ribbon. A five year old boy runs to the door, a look of excitement on his face.

"Uncle Les! Did you bring us gifts?"

"Paco, is that anyway to behave?"

Cohen puts down his packages and picks up Paco over his head. Paco spreads his arms like an airplane's wings. Cohen moves gracefully across the living room as Paco pretends to fly. Cohen carefully lands him onto a huge leather couch, as he sits down next to him. Esmerelda places a vase of beautiful red roses onto the nearby coffee table.

"You always bring me the most beautiful flowers."

"Beautiful flowers for a beautiful lady!" Esmerelda blushes as she goes over to pick up the other packages that Cohen had left by the door. She puts them next to Cohen on the sofa.

"So what did you and Aunt Ariana bring me?"

"This." Cohen hands Paco a rectangular gift wrapped box. Paco quickly unwraps it and opens the box. A look of disappointment on his face. "A shirt...."

"A shirt? This is an outrage! Well, perhaps this will make up for it?" Cohen hands Paco the remaining long, narrow box, identical to the one that had roses in it. Paco removes the ribbon and slowly opens the box. His face brightens immediately.

"A rifle! Look Mommy!" Paco takes the toy cowboy's rifle out and starts to point it at the full-size copy of the Venus di Milo near the bookcase. "Thank you Uncle Les. You're the best!" Paco hugs Cohen and kisses his cheek.

"I'm going to show this to Daddy!" Paco runs to the door, opens it and runs down the hallway, leaving the door open.

"You're always so kind." Esmerelda places a cup of coffee and a plate of fruit on the coffee table in front of him, and then sits next to him on his right.

"How is Paulina? How is she feeling?"

"Paulina is much better now thank God. She's sleeping now, very soundly."

"I'm so glad the doctor figured out what was wrong with her right away."

"I know. While TB is common in many parts of South America, here in San Mateo that's not been the case for over twenty years. I guess you could say that was one of the few good things Carlos Mendoza accomplished."

"Can I see her?"

"Of course." Cohen heads to Paulina's bedroom. Her crib is on the left side of the room, which is filled nearly wall to wall with toys and dolls. Cohen walks in quietly and comes to the side of the crib. He bends down and kisses her softly on the cheek. He unwraps the box and opens it to reveal a cute panda bear. He places it carefully next to her. Cohen walks out on his tiptoes to join Esmerelda, who's smiling at him by the doorway. They walk back together to the living room couch and sit down.

"You really love children. When are you and Ariana going to start a family?"

"As soon as Ariana let's me sleep with her."

Esmerelda cracks up with laughter. "Please. From what she tells me, I'm surprised that you don't have a dozen kids by now."

"I'm sure that Ariana exaggerates," as he winks to Esmerelda. "Oh my," as Cohen glances at his wristwatch,"where has the time gone. I better go see your husband before he gets jealous." Cohen kisses Esmerelda warmly on the lips before he gets off the couch.

"Well, we should at least give him reason too," as she lies back seductively on the couch.

"You are a naughty girl!"

"Perhaps you should let him win this time for a change…."

Moments later, Cohen walks out onto the magnificent palace garden. Sitting down at a table, sipping iced tea, is The General. In front of him is an ornate chess set, the pieces arranged to indicate the game has already been going on for some time now. The General has a big smile on his face when he sees that Cohen has arrived to continue their game. He gets up to greet him.

"General, it's so good to see you!" Cohen proceeds to shake The General's hand and embraces him warmly.

"So good to see you too. Please sit down. Enrique, bring Senor Cohen a rum and coke."

"Right away General."

"I'm so happy that Paulina is so much better now."

"Thank God for the Isoniazid."

"Yes, but she must take it religiously for a year, other wise she could have a relapse."

"I know. Problems with compliance is why TB will one day become resistant and perhaps untreatable."

Cohen smiles warmly to The General, a look of respect on his face. The General smiles warmly back to him.

"Paco loves his rifle. Thank you Les for all of your thoughtful gifts."

"De nada." Cohen is now looking over the chessboard, as The General observes him.

"Are you close to defeating me my friend?"

"I suspect I am, closer than you know." A slight smile is on Cohen's face.

"Oh really, then I'd better watch my ass!"

"Actually, you should be watching your queen." Cohen moves his knight in position to threaten both The General's king and queen. "Check."

The General's look turns to sudden anger. At that moment, Enrique returns with Cohen's drink.

"Shit! What is it Enrique?"

"Do you require anything else General?"

"No, now go away before I have you castrated!" Enrique quickly leaves, fear apparent on his face.

"Do you think I scared him?"

"I think he shitted in his pants."

"Good, I'm glad that I still have that effect on people."

"Oh, you haven't lost your touch sir, especially in chess."

"Fuck you Cohen!"

Cohen is nonplussed. "So what's your next move?"

"I guess I'll have to lose my queen to save myself."

"Unless you want to concede now?," a big smile on Cohen's face.

"Forget that compadre. Just drink your rum while I figure out how to get out of this mess." The General is looking over the chess board, apparently not getting much inspiration. He seems concerned to turn Cohen's attention to something else. A look of "Ah" touches The General's face.

"Tell me Les, what is it that you love about war?"

"General, a mercenary doesn't really fight for money. Sure, through your patronage I'm able to live the life of a modern day warlord, but I'd probably do it for free regardless. Your jungles remind me of Vietnam, and when I go out with my platoon now, I still get that feeling I knew back in Nam."

"What is that, power?"

"Not really, it's a natural high that's far more pervasive than what you could get from cocaine. When you're out there, facing the prospect that you might die that day, the realization of your mortality makes whatever time you have left that much more valuable. There's an excitement associated with the idea of kill or be killed that can not be overemphasized."

"Do you ever consider that you might be mentally disturbed because of Vietnam?"

"Oh, I'm pretty normal,", as he twitches and contorts his face. "General, I'm one of the lucky ones who was able to come back home after all I've done and seen. I was really fucked up when I got back to the States. You wouldn't have wanted to know me then."

"What are you talking about? I don't want to know you now!"

"Hey, fuck you.........sir." The General is trying to suppress his laughter. "Anyway, you know, the American people don't realize that the MIA's still left behind are better off in the jungle."

"Why is that?"

"The training in the Special Forces turned very young, impressionable men into barbaric killing machines. If the MIA's were brought back now, they most likely would end up shooting up a shopping mall, or snapping their wife's neck. Their minds are so distorted that they never could be integrated back into a normal life."

"Do you hate your country for that?"

"I hate them for selling us out, for not letting us finish what we started. And I didn't appreciate being spit on and called a baby killer when I came home. The American people had been lied to about the war, and so were the grunts who had to fight it."

"Well, I'm very glad that you feel at home in my country." The General pauses for a moment, as he sips from his iced tea. He finally moves his King over one space to his right. "You know, Rodriguez has volunteered to rid us of Father Lupe."

Cohen's face all of a sudden becomes very stern and serious. "Really, I'm shocked. I thought he was all for Lupe's quest for democratic reform."

"You never stop joking Amigo!"

"Actually, I believe your real enemy is much closer to home."

"What do you mean? Who would dare betray me?"

"Rodriguez, sir. As head of the Muertemos he has slowly been gaining more and more power and influence. The rich landowners don't fear you, isolated as you are in your palace, they fear Rodriguez. You've depended on him far too long, and it's probably only a short time before his next victim will be you."

"What do you have to gain by telling me this?"

"General, I'm happy with my life now. The lifestyle I've achieved through your patronage I could never obtain back in the States. I want to keep things as they are. I owe you and would be glad to take over Rodriguez's position."

"What do you propose?"

"When the time comes for your major assault against the resistance, I can arrange for his untimely death. But until such a time, I recommend that you pretend that this conversation never took place, or he will mount a coup' before we have time to defuse the situation."

"I will remain my normal, gregarious self! I will make no mistakes."

"I'm afraid you've already made a fatal one," as Cohen moves his Knight to capture The General's Queen, which then opens the path of Cohen's Queen to attack. "Check and mate!"

"You asshole!"

Chapter 3

As Cohen walks out the front of the Presidential Palace, Henry pulls up with his limo. Cohen opens up the door himself and sits next to Henry in the front. They proceed to drive out of the palace, and continue to pass through the uptown area. They slow down and stop on a street for a traffic light. As Cohen looks out to the left, he sees a bookstore named "EL GRAN LIBRE"....

San Mateo - 2 Years Ago

Cohen is running down the same uptown street and stops before a well established bookstore called "El Gran Libre". He checks his wristwatch. He looks into the storefront window and sees a photograph of a beautiful young woman. A sign next to it says "Poetry Reading/Book Signing by Ariana Leandre". Cohen comes in, picks up a copy of her new book and comes to the back of five rows of filled seats. In the front, the beautiful Ariana stands at a podium. The crowd has just finished clapping after a reading of hers. Her face is beaming at their response. As she looks towards the back of the audience, she notices the handsome Cohen standing, but then quickly looks away when he notices her gaze. Cohen raises his hand. "Miss Leandre."

"Please, call me Ariana."

He smiles to her. "Ariana, could you please recite 'Over a Windswept Shore'?"

"My goodness. That's from the first book I ever published. You know that?"

"Yes, it's my favorite."

"I'd be glad to." She pauses, as a look of nervousness comes to her face. "I'm so embarrassed. I forget how it starts. Could you help me?"

As sea gulls glide
Over a windswept shore, (in unison with Cohen)
Children listen well to
The stories an Old Man tells,
Of the seven seas, the exotic lands,

And then he draws their attention
To something in his hands,
A photograph, yellowed from age,
Of a woman, pretty yet plain,
Children, he said, don't go to sea,
For the glory that I gained from it
Wasn't worth the life it took from me,
The wife it took from me,
The life it took from me.

    The audience applauds both Ariana and Cohen, as he takes a slight bow. Ariana looks at Cohen with warmth and desire.
    Moments later, Cohen is waiting in line for Ariana to sign his book. As Ariana signs another person's book, Cohen appears to be smitten. His gaze lingers on her...
    "You were wonderful reciting Miss Leandre's poem," the woman behind him said.
    "What? Oh, thank you very much." Cohen finds it hard not to look at Ariana. When it's finally his turn, he almost trips over his own feet. (Under his breath) "That was real suave."
    "Hello! Who should I make out, I mean, dedicate this to?"
    "Les, Les Cohen."
    As she writes, "Do you write poetry yourself?"
    "I used to, long ago. But then I realized that not too many people, unfortunately, appreciate poetry. So I decided to write songs instead. Words, when you set them to music, are more likely to be heard and remembered. In that way, lyrics can sometimes have a more lasting and profound influence on people than poetry."
    "I'd love to hear your music...."
    Later that day, Cohen escorts Ariana to a bench in a nearby, beautiful public park. He takes his guitar out of its case and checks to see if it's in tune. He starts to serenade her....
Honey,
Why don't you come
Right over here,
Honey,
You got nothin,
Nothin to fear,
Even though I go out

Of my mind
Whenever you are near,

Listen,
To what I have
To say, I never,
Could find the way
To express my true feelin's
Until this very day,

Now I find, it's
Such a crime,
To search for many years,
With the fear
Of not finding
True love,
But now, I know
I found that
Love with you, oh
Even though it took
So long it doesn't
Matter at all, so

Honey,
Why don't you come
Right over here,
Honey,
You got nothin,
Nothin to fear,
Even though I go out
Of my mind,
Even though I go out
Of my mind, oh
Even though I go out
Of my mind
Whenever you are near!

    Ariana is very moved and impressed. She kisses Cohen gently on his neck....

Nacional Highway-10:23 AM, January 25th, 1979

A bump in the road jars Cohen back to the present. The two lane roadway has been under construction for some four years, and for most of the country still unfinished. But the part that runs towards Cohen's home and the other rich landowners in this area is for the most part complete. His limo now travels past elegant haciendas owned by his neighbors. Before reaching a fork in the road, Henry pulls off onto a private road lined with acacia trees. At the end of this pleasantly shaded road they finally reach the lush jungle plantation that is Cohen's home. The men guarding it appear to be American as well. As the car drives up to the front entrance, a beautiful young woman is seen looking through a body-length window above the entrance, a smile of joy apparent on her face.

Moments later, Cohen walks into his bedroom, apparently looking for someone. Suddenly he's grabbed from behind.

"Got you!" Cohen turns around and embraces his woman warmly. "Why did you take so long? I was worried about you." Ariana starts to kiss him passionately.

"I'm sorry Darling. I had to speak to a doctor," as he starts to fondle her small, firm breasts.

"What's wrong, are you ill?"

"No, no, don't worry. I was asking the good doctor to help others in need. In fact, you will meet him this evening."

"Oh, so you will be too busy today?"

"Why, what do you have in mind?" He starts to kiss her neck, which made her feel very aroused. He starts to grab her tight ass.

"Well, I thought you could..."

"Sing you a new song?"

Ariana gives a mock disappointed look. He rushes over to grab his guitar leaning on the wall. Ariana follows right behind him. He looks back to see a very mischievous look on her face. He turns back to get his guitar when she reaches around to gently grab his instrument. He turns around to start to kiss her again, as she moves close to massage him.

"I guess I'll sing it to you later."

"You'd better."

He gently pushes her to the bed and has her sit down near the edge. He slowly starts to kiss the inside of her left leg, starting near the ankle, then slowly moves up her calf and knee.

"Keep going."

He continues to kiss her, moving up her thigh until he remembers to remark: "You're sure you don't want to hear my song now?"

"Later damn it!"

"Okay. Now where was I? Oh yes..." Cohen continues to kiss and lick her gently as he moves further up, till she soon moans: "I want you now."

We hear him pull down his pants, as he climbs on top of her and begins.......

Muertemos Interrogation Cell-10:53 AM, January 25th, 1979

Dr. Aramos is seen next to the peristaltic pump. He is covered with blood, as are the three men he has just finished with. They can be heard sobbing very weakly. Aramos flips the on-off switch several times before coming to the conclusion that it doesn't work. "I don't want to disappoint my new sponsor." Aramos opens his mouth to reveal his glistening fangs. The Muertemos look back in disbelief and then horror.

Cohen's and Ariana's Bedroom-10:53 AM

Ariana is sitting on top of Cohen now, rhythmically moving up and down till she finishes, and then gently moves off of him, to lie next to him as he embraces her. "Did you enjoy that?"

"Very much, but I would like some more if you please?"

"Let me catch my breath. Why don't you play me your song while I recuperate?"

"Good idea. I hope you like it." Cohen bounds out naked to get his guitar. He gets back into bed, sitting Indian style before her and begins to sing:

Walking down the street,
Hand in hand,
You are my woman,
And I'm your man,

Oh how I need you,
To stand by my side,
Cause I really trust you,
With my feelin's
I normally hide,

Seems just like a dream,
From the very start,
I never thought I,
Could win your heart,

Oh how I want you,
To hold me, So tight,
And how I miss you,
When you leave me,
Late at night,
Oh how I want you,
To hold me, So tight,
And how I miss you,
When you leave me,
Late at night,
Oh how I miss you,
When you leave me,
Late at night!

Ariana gets up to embrace him tightly, tears running down her cheeks.

Muertemos Interrogation Cell-10:56 AM, January 25th, 1979

Dr. Aramos bangs on the door. The Muertemos standing guard opens the door, but it's partly blocked by Aramos. "I'm finished with my work. It's time for me to wash up before you take me to Cohen." Aramos starts to leave the cell. "If I were you, I wouldn't look in there."

The guard brushes him aside and pushes the door completely open. We see his face as he looks around, and he bends over and starts to vomit. He quickly closes the cell and looks at Aramos with shock, quickly moving back away from him.

"I told you not to look."

"Pedro", wiping his mouth from the vomit, "come take the doctor to wash up. Then have him brought to Mr. Cohen."

Pedro is shocked by the look on the guard's face, and begins to escort Aramos to their shower room. All of the guards at the cell doors along the hallway unconsciously moved their hands to their pistols as Aramos walks by, the hair on the back of their necks standing up. They don't dare to take their eyes off of Aramos as he passes by each one of them.

Chapter 4

Cohen's Plantation Office-6:42 PM, January 25th, 1979

Cohen is sitting at his desk in his home's office. He is holding a Ninja star. He turns it in a circular fashion in his right hand. As he looks at it more closely, he begins to have a flashback.....

North Vietnamese Jungle-August 13th, 1970

A 23 year old Cohen, with hair grown below shoulder length, is sleeping on a tree branch high off the ground. A wild rat snuggles next to him as it sleeps as well. In the Special Forces, the men are taught to use nature to their advantage in war, as were the Ninja centuries before. The wild rat is not the same as their city-dwelling cousins. They're friendly to humans and seek them out for warmth at night. When the rat suddenly wakes up and scurries away, Cohen is brought to consciousness. The full moon shines in his open eyes directly above, as he hears the cries of an American in the distance.

At a nearby river, a Vietcong captain is struggling to hold the American POW's head under the water, as he laughs with glee. The seven other POWs are enraged. Their hands are tied behind their backs and a rope connects them all together by their necks. The two other Vietcong join in their captain's laughter. The Vietcong captain suddenly pulls the American's head out of the water, and lays him down on his back [his hands also are tied behind him] next to the river's edge. The American coughs up water. A look of surprise is seen on the other POW's faces. The other Vietcong know better and are smirking. The American starts to come to. The VC captain takes some deep drags on a cigarette he just lit, as he waits for the POW to be fully conscious. As the American looks into his eyes, the VC Captain slowly pulls out a sword and shows it to the POW to taunt him. He suddenly presses down hard with his right hand on the POW's forehead, who starts to struggle to move away. The VC captain lifts up his sword and then hacks away several times before the American's head comes off. The other POWs start to run towards the VC captain, but his two lieutenants move in their way and point their machine guns at them. The VC captain puts the American's head into a knapsack attached to his belt. He kicks the limp body into the river.

"Let's go. I want to get to dinner on time," the Vietcong captain orders. The two other VC motion with their machine guns to get the remaining POWs to move out. One VC lieutenant walks closely with his captain up front, while the other stays behind the POWs. They all move towards the tree that Cohen is in.

Cohen is now crouched low on his branch, as he watches the VC and the POWs pass by under him. When the VC in the rear finally passes by, he doesn't notice a makeshift noose of vine lowered right before his head. As soon as his head is caught, Cohen begins to pull him up to the branch. The VC is clutching his throat, unable to cry out. Cohen jumps backward off his branch, pulling the rope with him, as he rappels downward. The vine slides against the tree branch. Cohen lands silently on the ground, using the vine and the VC's weight as a pulley to slow his descent. He ties the end of the rope to an exposed root and then quickly falls in with the POWs, keeping his hands behind his back. The VC captain soon stops, looking back to speak with his other lieutenant. "Wei Lo, where are you?"

The lieutenant up front looks further back and is seized with horror when he suddenly sees his comrade hanging from the branch. He starts to point, "Captain......," but before he can continue, a whizzing sound is heard as a spinning, flashing Ninja star rips through the air and lodges in his throat. He starts to spurt blood and gurgle, trying desperately to pull it out of his throat. The VC captain looks on with horror and then starts to point his machine gun towards the POWs. Before he has the chance to pull the trigger, Cohen is seen flinging another Ninja star in one smooth motion. The Ninja star hits the VC captain in his forehead, knocking him down on his back. As he regains his consciousness, we see Cohen walking over to him, taking out a 20 inch sword of his own. As he smiles down to the VC captain, he proceeds to step hard on the VC's groin. When the VC jerks his head up due to the pain of his crushed testicles, Cohen decapitates him with a single strike. The POWs are looking at him with amazement, as he place's the VC's head into a knapsack of his own. Cohen then walks over to the POWs, cutting the ropes binding them with his blood-drenched sword.......

Cohen's Plantation Office-6:43 PM, January 25th, 1979

"Les, Dr. Aramos is here."

Cohen is startled for a moment, as he is jarred back into the present. For the moment he has a surprised look on his face, for he doesn't recognize the clean shaven, handsome man for the Aramos he knew before.

"Thank you Victor, that will be all."

"Yes sir," as the tall, muscular man closes the door behind him.

"Please Dr. Aramos, have a seat." Aramos sits down in a plush chair before Cohen's desk.

"Cigarette?"

"No thank you. Those will kill you one day."

"In my line of work, I doubt if I'll be around long enough for that to matter. Anyway doctor, how do you feel?"

"While I worked on my "patients", I felt really good having revenge. But ultimately, it makes no difference, since my Luisa still is dead."

"I'm sorry for that. I know from experience that that type of revenge still leaves you hollow, but without it, a person is eaten up inside anyway." Aramos appears uncomfortable. "Anyway, were you able to comply with my request?"

"Yes, the procedure went smoothly."

"Thank you doctor, I knew you could do it if properly motivated."

"I met your Ariana at your front door. She's a beautiful lady."

"Thank you. I don't know if you realize it, but it was your brother who presided over our marriage?"

"Yes, he told me. Does it bother you that you didn't marry within your religion?"

"Not at all. I married for love. To me, most religious beliefs are just a bunch of horseshit. I'd sooner trust a sincere atheist than a born again idiot."

"You mean to say that you don't believe in God."

"That's a strange comment from someone who has every reason not to believe. But yes, I do believe God exists. Why he allows the innocent on Earth to be fucked over, I'll never understand."

"That's a strange comment from someone who helped The General do just that."

"Dr. Aramos, I'm not responsible for The General's actions, nor for his scumbag Rodriguez's Muertemos. I've done things in my life that I'm not very proud of, but I never killed anyone who didn't have the chance to kill me as well. Yes, I did help The General come to power, and I obviously still benefit from his patronage, but I'm here now to offer you, Father Lupe and your people a way to get your country back in your own hands." Cohen reaches under his desk for a backpack and places it on his desk. He opens it and pulls out a Kevlar bulletproof vest and an IV bag filled with blood.

"Dr. Aramos, you'll give your brother this vest to wear, before he begins Sunday Mass. On top of it, underneath his shirt, he'll also have this bag of blood to give the right effect."

"Are you sure you won't miss?"

"My good doctor, in Nam I was an assassin for the Special Forces. I never failed on any of my missions. Ironically, this is the first time my aim will not be to kill my target, only to martyr him temporarily. You'll also find rope in here that you'll need to strategically place for him to grab onto. My associate Victor will help you with that when he brings you back to Jualape tonight after dinner."

"I'll do whatever it takes to ensure my brother's safety."

"Of that I have no doubt. Also, Victor will provide you with the peristaltic pump as well, which should be arriving later. He will fit it with a battery pack for your convenience."

"I don't understand."

"I'm sorry. You will need to perform some fieldwork tomorrow at Jualape. I hope to provide you with at least one "patient" to drain."

"I will not kill any innocent people."

"You need not worry about that. Just make sure that it looks like nosferatu did it."

"Nosferatu?"

"Yes, nosferatu. It's another term for the undead."

"Ah, why didn't you just say a vampire?"

"Jesus, I just like the sound of ....nosferatu!"

(Under his breath) "Schmuck."

"I heard that."

"Mr. Cohen...."

"Please, call me Les."

"Alright, Les, I was hoping you could help me to find someone." Dr. Aramos pulls out a small piece of folded paper from his pocket and hands it to Cohen. Cohen's eyes brighten when he sees the name.

"Are you Jewish Aramos?"

"No, should I drop my pants for you to check my penis?"

"No, I just ate. I'd rather just believe you. You realize that the Israelis have been looking for this asswipe for over thirty years."

"I'm sure the Mossad, as well as the CIA has been less than successful with the German communities down here, but an inquiry made for his well compensated consultantship, required by a repressive South American regime's project to eliminate their Mestizo population would be more likely to garner success. Forgive my suggestion, since I realize that Ariana is Mestizo."

"No need doctor, and I believe your idea actually might work, since I believe this piece of shit did the very same thing in Paraguay years ago. While I consider him normally less than worthless, I'll have Rodriguez make the inquiries, since no one would question his sincerity in such a matter."

"Thank you Les," as Aramos looks pleased at last.

Muertemos Interrogation Center-7:10 PM, January 25th, 1979

Colonel Rodriguez walks up to the guard, who is startled when Rodriguez speaks to him: "What's wrong? You look like you saw a ghost."

"No Colonel, I saw something much worse."

"Buck up man, you call yourself a Muertemos. Now open the door." The guard hesitates, then proceeds to let Rodriguez in. Rodriguez walks into the cell that Aramos had worked in. As soon as he sees his handiwork, he turns back and proceeds to vomit on the guard who followed right behind him.

"Are you alright Colonel?", as he tries to hide his look of disgust.

"I thought you were playing a trick on me." The Colonel slowly turns back to see the three dead Muertemos, still tied down to their gurneys. They are nearly white from their blood being completely drained. Their crotches are missing both testicles and penises, which Aramos left beside their heads. Their arms have been chopped off, close to their shoulders. All the wounds were cauterized to prevent them from bleeding to death until Aramos was ready to drain them. Their abdomens have been slit open and then stitched expertly. Rodriguez has a puzzled look on his face, until he sees their intestines piled up in the corner of the room. He has seen enough.

"I want these bodies and all their remains to be removed and cremated now."

"Yes Colonel, right away."

"And have all the instruments and pump returned to Cohen right away as well." Rodriguez leaves without another word. The other guards by their doors don't dare to look at him in his agitated state.

Presidential Office-7:26 PM, January 25th, 1979

Rodriguez holds the glass of wine in his hand, as his eyes roll across The General's office, done in French provincial decor. He still looks pale from what he has just seen.

"What's wrong Sanchez? Don't you like my Bordeaux? I feel insulted."

"I'm sorry General, I'm just a little under the weather." Rodriguez meekly takes a sip, holding back an urge to vomit. "Very good Bordeaux, General.", he belches.

"Lets face it, you wouldn't know a fine wine from bottled piss."

The color starts to come back to Rodriguez's face, as well as a smile, upon hearing The General's remark.

"That may be so, but what do I care? Just give me my money, my position, and lots of whores!"

"But not in that order."

"After all that we've been through, you know my priorities." Since Rodriguez is staring at the wine in his glass, he doesn't see the brief look of anger The General lets slip through.

"I know that your middle initials are V.D.."

"Excuse me while I throw up."

"Before you do, what's the status of Father Lupe?"

Rodriguez's eyes brighten, as he sits up to speak. "General, Lupe is going too far. My offer still stands. It would be an honor to snuff him out."

"I agree also that he has gone too far, but you are not to kill him." A look of surprise and worry is apparent on Rodriguez's face. "I don't want your Muertemos to appear to be involved, so I agreed with Cohen to let him do it. I believe you'd agree that he's an expert assassin."

"Why yes, General." Rodriguez finds it hard to hide his disappointment and concern.

"He's going to take him out after Sunday Mass in Jualape. Make sure nothing gets in his way."

"Yes General."

Cohen's Plantation Office-7:32 PM, January 25th, 1979

Cohen's right hand man, Victor, comes in after knocking on the door. "Les, Ariana wants you to know that dinner will be ready in ten minutes."

"Thank you Victor. Dr. Aramos, please go refresh your self. We'll start dinner as soon as you're ready."

"Thank you," as Aramos gets up and leaves with Victor.

Cohen looks at the name on the sheet of paper Aramos had given him once more, as he smiles to himself. He picks up his phone's receiver and dials.

"Captain Suarez."

"Yes Mr. Cohen."

"Patch me in to Colonel Rodriguez."

"Yes, at once."

Cohen's Dining Room-7:42 PM-January 25th, 1979

The dinning table is set for three. Ariana is very happy to see Dr. Aramos again.

"Dr. Aramos, please sit here next to me."

"Please, call me Hector." Aramos sits at the head of the table, followed by Ariana on his left.

"Alright, Hector. Tell me, how is your dear brother?"

Aramos finds it hard to hide his concern. "He would say that he's fine, but I fear for his safety."

"I know, I do as well. He is a great man, a good man who tells the truth. Unfortunately, such men are always feared by those in power." A big smile is seen on Aramos's face for the first time. Ariana misunderstands the gesture. "Did I say something stupid?"

"Forgive me, not at all. It's just that hearing you talk like that reminded me of my daughter Luisa. She shared your love of justice but..."

"But what? Please, you can open your heart to me."

"She paid with her life for her convictions. She spoke as you do now when she was attending college. I warned her to be silent. She wanted to help my brother's cause by bringing his message to her fellow students but was betrayed by one of her closest friends."

"That's horrible. Why would they do such a thing?"

"Her so called friend was jealous of Luisa because of her boyfriend, a boy she desired. So she notified the police of Luisa's activities, who then had the Muertemos...," he hesitates, with tears in his throat, "they had them rape and murder her."

"My God, I knew what happened to your Luisa but not the reason why. Father Lupe told me no one knew why. Are you sure?"

"Yes, yes. I only learned today the truth, but I can't tell you how I found out." At that moment, Cohen arrives to the dining room.

"Please forgive me. My telephone conversation took much longer than I thought."

"That's alright, I'm very glad to be able to speak to Ariana."

"Mandalena, please bring us the soup," Cohen called out.

"Yes senor Cohen."

"Where is the girl now that betrayed Luisa?," Ariana asked.

"She had committed suicide soon after Luisa's murder. Now I realize that when Luisa's boyfriend must have rejected her, her sense of guilt drove her to that. And to think I bothered to go to her funeral, that I tried to comfort her parents."

Ariana looks very sad and doesn't know what to say. Cohen pours sangria into their glasses, starting with Ariana's, followed by Aramos's, then finally his.

"Anyway, life must go on. I must hope for a better world to come or I will go mad."

"You're a good man Hector. Here's to good health and happiness for all our loved ones, and for success to our goal for the people of San Mateo!" Cohen exclaimed. They all toast to this warmly.

"Les, if we are successful, one day you may find yourself in the history books!"

"That would not be my first choice, since I don't want the CIA after my ass for spoiling their plans in this region." With that, Mandalena comes in with the soup.

"Good, I don't know about you but I'm starving."

"I'm amazed that you can eat with what you face tomorrow."

Cohen shoots an angry glance at Aramos. He sees that Ariana is worried. "Ariana, please don't let the good doctor alarm you. I do need to leave tonight to do some important work. I should be back by tomorrow evening."

"Darling, you told me you would not do any more dangerous work."

"I will be just fine. Now let's just enjoy our dinner." With that, Ariana gets up to leave, her eyes are moist with the beginning of tears.

"Forgive me Hector, I need to get some air." Ariana then walks out to the back patio.

"Forgive me for my big mouth. But I thought she knew that you are helping Juan."

"Yes, that's true. But she has no idea of the nature of my help. Doctor, I apologize because you're not used to this. Ariana obviously knows that I'm not a traveling salesman, but I still never reveal to her what I do in my work. That way, I protect her from those who would want to extract information about me. By leaving her in the dark is one of the best ways I can protect her."

"As would the head of a crime family."

"Precisely. Now if you'll excuse me, I need to apologize to my wife."

"By all means."

"Mandalena, please attend to the doctor's every wish."
"Yes senor."

Cohen walks out to the patio, which is surrounded by a lush garden. He finds Ariana crying on a patio chair next to a large in ground swimming pool.

"Ariana, there's no need to cry. You know that I am helping Father Lupe, but there are things I must do to accomplish that, things you must understand that I have to keep secret from you. I know that there shouldn't be secrets between a man and wife, but I also know that I never want anything bad to happen to you. I never thought I would ever marry because of the work I do. You changed my mind about that, and I will do whatever I have to do to protect you always."

"You're a dangerous man to love, but there's no one else I would ever want to be with."

Cohen embraces her passionately. He looks deeply into her eyes. "Then kiss me you fool!"

Ariana cracks up at that. She proceeds to kiss him with obvious joy.

"Now let's go back to join the good doctor before the food gets cold."

"You animal, do you always have your mind on eating?"

"Yes, but what I enjoy eating most is only served by you." Ariana gives an embarrassed, knowing smile.

"You naughty boy!" As they walk back Cohen playfully grabs her ass.

Cohen's Plantation -9:43 PM, January 25th, 1979

Cohen and Ariana are with Dr. Aramos in the foyer. "Well Hector, thank you for joining us for dinner."

"No, thank you Ariana, for the pleasure has been all mine." Ariana comes to Aramos and warmly embraces him and kisses him on the cheek.

"You are always welcome in our home Hector. Vaya con Dios!" Aramos is very moved by this.

"Ariana, I am sure that your parents would be very proud of you, as I am now! Now I'd better go before I get too emotional."

"Good night Hector." Cohen and Aramos leave through the front door, and walk to a jeep Victor is waiting in.

"Victor, take good care of Dr. Aramos and Father Lupe for me."

"You got it sir."

"And you have everything they'll need for tomorrow?"

"Yes sir." Aramos sits in the passenger seat as Victor begins to slowly drive round the circular driveway. Ariana waves enthusiastically to Aramos, and Aramos waves back in turn.

"She's a fine young lady."

"You're right about that doctor." The guard opens the gate to let them out, as Victor gets back onto the tree-lined road in front of Cohen's plantation. Once he's on the Nacional Highway, he proceeds to pass by the full length of Cohen's land and continues to drive past several more neighbor's haciendas. As the highway almost comes to an abrupt end, Victor turns south onto a dirt road. The sound of cicadas fill the air, as the forest becomes denser.

"Excuse me, Victor. If you don't mind me asking, why do you work for Mr. Cohen?"

"Well Dr. Aramos, some nine years ago I was a POW in North Vietnam. One night, after a Major John Hackett was brutally murdered by our captors near a river, Mr. Cohen rescued us single handedly. When we got back to the States, we made sure that he would get recognition for what he had done for us. We petitioned our senators and Mr. Cohen received the Congressional Medal of Honor. We kept in touch, and when he called asking for men to join him to fight in San Mateo, me, Henry, Paul, and friends of ours as well came to work under his command."

"He is a brave man, and a great leader to elicit such devotion in his men."

"I would die for Les Cohen."

"Let's hope that it doesn't have to come to that." Victor will need to keep maneuvering around potholes and fallen branches on their way to Jualape.....

Chapter 5

Cohen's Plantation Office-12:02 AM, January 26th, 1979

Cohen is now dressed in camouflage pants, muscle shirt and his face painted with green and black bands diagonally across it. He goes to a wall panel behind his desk and pushes it gently inward. It springs back and he pulls it open, revealing a small room. Flipping on a series of fluorescent lights, one sees the storeroom contains a collection of various rifles, pistols, swords, knives and Ninja stars. He removes an M21 Sniper rifle, several extra clips for it and then leaves the room after switching off the lights, and closes its paneled entrance.

He leaves through a double glass door leading to a balcony, from which he silently climbs down a thick grapevine along the side of his home to the grass below. His Harley is leaning on the wall nearby. He walks his motorcycle down a path till he reaches the edge of trees, when he then straddles it and kicks the Harley into life. He speeds away through the trees till he reaches a clearing on his plantation where his Huey helicopter is kept. When Henry sees him, he starts it up. Cohen gets on and they arc up as they whisk away into the night.

"Henry, drop me off about a click south of Jualape."

"Will you need anyone besides Victor to back you up sir?"

"I don't think so, but stay by the radio in case something strange should come up."

"Most definitely sir." The helicopter continues its low flight over the rain forest's canopy. When the sparse lights of Jualape could be seen, Henry starts to circle gently to look for a possible drop off point.

"How about here sir?"

"This will be fine." Cohen went back to the rear cabin area and slides open the side door. After securing his rifle and accessories, he lowers himself down a rope. Once he is clear he gives Henry the thumbs up to winch it up. Once the rope is safely retracted, Henry continues to fly towards Jualape. He passes right over the village before flying into a ravine adjacent to Jualape's church. He flies about two miles before he finds a suitable, secluded spot to land. Once on the ground, as the rotors are slowly winding down, we see him take out a large, dog-eared novel to read.

Back at Jualape, Cohen is making his way to the edge of the village near where the church is located. At the edge of the tree line, around two thousand feet away, he starts to climb a huge Banyon tree. Finding a suitable branch high above the ground, we see him settling in for the night.

Village of Jualape-9:30 AM, January 26th, 1979

Father Lupe is waiting near the front of the simple church, shaking the hands of his parishioners. A look of joy is on his face as he converses with them. Dr. Aramos is standing nearby, and starts to walk with him as Father Lupe begins to walk along the edge of the ravine. Fellow parishioners are walking nearby, as their children start to play games. A jeep suddenly screeches to a halt nearby, followed by three Muertemos leaving it as they approach the crowd.

"Father Lupe, we've been told that a plot has been made against your life. We're here to take you to a safe place." said the first Muertemos.

"I'll be just fine. There's no need to be concerned. Please thank Colonel Rodriguez for the thought, though."

A look of concern and skepticism is on the faces of the crowd. The first Muertemos moves towards the left side of the parishioners, who have formed a large semi-oval around the area, Father Lupe and Dr. Aramos at its center, near the edge of the ravine. The second Muertemos is near the central edge while the third Muertemos moves to the right side within it. They show no fear, expecting no villager to dare attack them.

The first Muertemos is starting to get pissed off. "I was not requesting you, this is an order. Or perhaps you need some incentive?" The first Muertemos goes over to a nearby teenage girl and grabs her by the arm. He drags her towards his original position. "I'll just take her along with us to guarantee your cooperation."

"That won't be necessary, I'll do as you bid. Now let her go." Father Lupe pleads.

"I don't think so. My men and I need to have some fresh pussy, isn't that right Jorge?

"That's right Miguel, we haven't had a four-way for at least a month."

All three of the Muertemos start laughing as the first one starts to cup the girl's right breast in his hand. She shrieks and tries to get away. The first Muertemos grabs her by her hair as we see Dr. Aramos, his face cold like stone, starting to move towards him.

"No Hector!" Father Lupe warns.

The first Muertemos points his pistol at Dr. Aramos. "Don't be an asshole, old man." The next moment the crack of a rifle fills the air, as the first Muertemos is shot in the head, his blood and brains splattering on the teenage girl. Before there's time to react, Father Lupe is shot in the heart, as he's knocked over and falls into the ravine. Father Lupe is sliding down the ravine's slope, trying to grab the rope strung along to catch him. He just misses it. But a moment later Victor grabs him and pulls him under a rock ledge.

The second Muertemos runs towards the ravine's edge. He looks over to see a body at the bottom, dressed just like Father Lupe. As he turns around Dr. Aramos is right in front of him, as he pushes the second Muertemos backwards into the ravine. The Muertemos tumbles backwards, and is stopped suddenly when his leg gets caught in a tree branch. He ends up hanging headfirst. He can't lift himself up and is trapped in this position.

Up above, the third Muertemos starts to blindly shoot his rifle towards where he thought Cohen has shot from. Again we hear a single crack as Cohen shoots him in the leg, giving him only a flesh wound. He starts running away with a limp, as we see Dr. Aramos running very nimbly after him.

The other parishioners come to the edge of the ravine and see the prostrate body of "Father Lupe" on the bottom. They all start to weep and cross themselves. Cohen starts shooting above their heads, causing them to scramble away for cover.

Moments later, nearly exhausted, the third Muertemos is seen limping into a barn, closes the door and makes his way to the back and falls down onto a hill of straw. He soon hears someone knocking on the barn door and immediately shoots several times in its direction. Dr. Aramos proceeds to open the door and walks in.

"Please, let me help you. I'm a doctor."

The third Muertemos is stunned, for he sees that Aramos had been shot in the chest. "What the hell are you? I shot you, why aren't you dead?"

Dr. Aramos looks surprised at his comment, and then looks down to see the hole in his shirt. A ring of blood is seen around the bullet hole. He tears open his shirt to reveal the bleeding wound as it slowly closes itself up and the blood disappears from his skin. The Muertemos looks in awe and then his awe turns to fear as Dr. Aramos looks directly at him, his glistening fangs revealed as he smiles towards him.

"I guess I lied about wanting to help you." Aramos runs towards the Muertemos and picks him off the ground by clutching his groin in one hand, and his throat in the other. He proceeds to squeeze his groin hard, as the Muertemos cries out in agony. "Let me educate you!" as he sinks his teeth into his neck.

Moments later, the second Muertemos is shocked to see that Father Lupe is alive and well, walking down the ravine's slope with a huge man beside him. He tries once again to lift up his torso to free his leg from the branch, almost reaches the branch with his right hand, and then falls back to find Dr. Aramos' face upside down and in front of his.

"Did you see that, Father Lupe is still alive?!"

"Isn't it wonderful!?," as he sinks his fangs greedily into his neck.

Village of Jualape-12:46 PM, January 26th, 1979

Colonel Rodriguez and Cohen are seen near the edge of Jualape's ravine. Rodriguez's platoon forms a semi - circle around them. Cohen agilely climbs down, while Rodriguez follows slowly down the slope, using a rope for support. Rodriguez looks very uncomfortable doing this.

The sound of flies are deafening as they come to the hanging corpse of the second Muertemos.

"Who is it?," Cohen asks

"It's Jorge," as he brushes the flies away from the body. His flesh is white like milk. A look of horror falls upon the four other Muertemos that had followed them down.

"Hey, put him in a body bag and take him and the other one to the morgue on the double," Rodriguez orders.

"Yes sir," the nearest Muertemos replies.

Rodriguez then takes Cohen aside to talk. "The General will not like this," Rodriguez whispers.

"I know," Cohen smirks. "And if things go as we plan, you'll soon take his place Sanchez."

Rodriguez shows a shark-like grin upon hearing this. "That Aramos does damn good work. It's almost a shame that you'll have to kill Lupe for real once this is over."

"All in good time Sanchez. We need Aramos's cooperation till you've taken over; then I'll do them both."

"Alright," Rodriguez pauses, "it's best that I escort the bodies back and supervise the autopsies personally."

"Let me know when we should meet with The General," as Cohen walks away down the slope.

Chapter 6

Presidential Palace-6:06 PM, January 26th, 1979

A flaming setting sun filters through the window behind him. The General sits behind his ornate desk. He takes long drags on his cigar, a smile of contentment on his face. His reverie is broken by the sudden buzzing of his intercom.

"General, Colonel Rodriguez and Mr. Cohen are here to see you," The General's secretary informs.

"Send them right in Adolpho."

The two men come in and sit on the two Louis XIV chairs in front of his desk. The General offers both of them a cigar, which they both decide to indulge in. They light up and take several puffs before The General begins.

"You know, I had a visit earlier today from an envoy of the CIA. President Carter has offered me their protection should I desire. It does my heart good to know that the United States still favors the existence of oppressive regimes like ours, as long as they're not communist! In fact, I'm so pleased with their offer that even this coroner's report on my desk doesn't upset me too much. However, I'd like to know how three of your best men died at Jualape."

"Well sir, actually Cohen is responsible for one of the deaths."

"Oh really, why is that Les?"

Cohen gives a menacing glance towards Rodriguez. "General, one of his asshole subordinates was in my line of fire. He shouldn't have been there in the first place."

The General turns red as he bangs his desk, and then looks towards Rodriguez with dagger eyes. "Why the fuck were your men there at all?"

"General, you told me that you didn't want the Muertemos to be implicated in Lupe's assassination. What better way to do that than to have them there supposedly to safeguard his existence?"

"I now see why they say that genius has its limits, but stupidity doesn't! Your "brilliant" idea almost ruined my mission, you shit for brains."

"General, I don't have to sit here and be insulted like this. What if the Jew boy and I were to go outside and settle this once and for all, mano a mano?"

"Cohen would kill you, so you should thank me that I won't let you try." The General proceeds to flick the ashes from his cigar hard, missing his ashtray and landing on Rodriguez's pants. Cohen has a big smile on his face.

Rodriguez is trying hard to conceal his embarrassment and hate.

"Now tell me, what happened to your other men that Cohen didn't kill?" The General asks sarcastically.

"Sir, both of the men died from an extreme loss of blood. Two incisive marks were found in their carotid artery."

"You mean their neck?"

"Yes General, it's all in the report."

The General leafs through it, stopping two-thirds the way through. "It mentions that the man they found in the barn, Roberto Mantez, that his testicles were crushed."

"Well, at least Rodriguez would be immune to such treatment!" Cohen quips.

"Fuck you Cohen!"

"Shut your hole Sanchez." The General orders. The General leafs through the pages till he found the conclusion. "Dr. Fuentes reports that the punctures were made by canine teeth, but not from any known animal."

"Yes, he found the distance between the punctures would be too large to be made by a wolf or wild dog, and too small for larger carnivores. Yet, the distance is just right for an average human," Cohen interjects.

"Cohen, that's absurd. Do you expect me to believe in such claptrap?"

"General, I don't believe in vampires or any other superstitions, but something killed those men."

"Couldn't a person with medical training perform such a task Les?"

"One shouldn't rule that out, but the speed with which it occurred would be difficult to replicate with a pump system."

"What did either of you learn from the villagers?"

"Not surprisingly, no one would confide to Sanchez." Rodriguez glances back with a pissed off look. "Some of the elders came forward to tell me what they knew. They informed me that Father Lupe had made arrangements in case he should meet an untimely death." Cohen pauses, tapping his fingers on his chair's arms.

"Well, go on."

"They said that Father Lupe summoned a lackey of the Devil to fulfill his curse on anyone responsible for his death."

"That's correct sir. One of my men who heard his recent speech would testify to that," Rodriguez adds.

"Is that all you have for me? I should have sent my five year old to investigate this mess."

"No, that's not all sir," Cohen replied.

"Oh really, what else can you educate me about?"

"Father Lupe's body is missing."

A look of fear is briefly seen on The General's face. "What do you mean?"

"The villagers had seen his body after I shot him at the bottom of the ravine. However, by the time Rodriguez and I had gotten there, his body was gone."

The General gets up and walks to his globe, gazing down at the South American continent.

"General, whatever or whoever the murderer is, that doesn't matter. What does matter is that you must be protected." Cohen warned.

"Cohen is right, General. You must not make any speeches or leave the palace until we settle this matter."

The General gazes lovingly at the globe for a brief moment, as if lost in thought. He then turns and looks at Cohen and Rodriguez, his face cold and emotionless.

"Rodriguez, Jualape must burn." The General orders. A moment of silence fills the office.

"I will go there with my men around 3:00 AM, to catch them while they're all disoriented. That's something I heard that Stalin had his KGB do as standard practice." Rodriguez replied.

"I didn't realize you were a fucking student of history." Cohen observed, as Rodriguez's anger was reaching its breaking point. Then Cohen looked directly at The General:

"What's to be done with the villagers, sir? The children?" Cohen asked.

"I said Jualape must burn, that means with everything in it."

"I just wanted to make sure how far you wanted to take this." Cohen and Rodriguez get up to leave, and are almost out the door when The General warns,

"In case this lackey does exist, you both should be careful, since we all had a hand in Lupe's demise, most directly you Les."

"Thanks for the concern General. Are you wearing a crucifix, sir?"

"Why no, should I be?"

"It couldn't hurt."

Cohen and Rodriguez leave The General's office. Inside The General has a look of concern on his face, as he leafs through the coroner's report once more, feeling his neck unconsciously as he reads it.

Moments later, as Cohen and Rodriguez are seen leaving the front entrance of the palace, they appear to be suppressing the urge to crack up from laughter. It takes them a moment to catch their breath.

"I think that went very well." Cohen whispers.

Rodriguez whispers back "The General looked really worried. I almost feel sorry for him. There's one thing that bothers me though."

"Really? What's that?"

"You know Les, you didn't have to be so harsh to me in front of The General."

"Jeez, I didn't realize that you were so fucking sensitive. Sanchez, I simply had to give a convincing performance. We can't afford for The General to have the slightest doubt that we hate each other."

"I'm sorry, of course you're right."

"Of course I am." A palace guard is now passing within listening distance of Cohen and Rodriguez.

Cohen now yells out loud "Now get lost you flaming prick!"

"One day you'll pay for all the shit you pull on me you Jew bastard!" Rodriguez bellows back, and then he saunters off.

"Such a schmuck." Cohen says under his breath, and then proceeds to give him the finger.

Chapter 7

Muertemos Locker Room-1:35 AM, January 27th, 1979

A rank locker room. Some twenty men are getting into fatigues. They check their pistols and rifles. A man is silently praying near his locker, holding the crucifix around his neck tightly. Other men see him and do the same.

"What's up with them? Why the sudden conversion?" a young Muertemos asks.

"Didn't you hear what happened at Jualape?" an old Muertemos replies.

"No old man."

"Well then, let's just say I'd rather not go." The old Muertemos takes a huge crucifix from his locker and puts it around his neck. The men nearby overhear him and nod in agreement.

Village of Jualape-2:56 AM, January 27th, 1979

Rodriguez is seen standing in a jeep positioned on a hill overlooking the center of Jualape. His driver Manuel is sitting in the driver's seat, the engine running. Rodriguez is looking through night vision binoculars as he sees two Muertemos approaching the orphanage.

These two Muertemos, one carrying a can of gasoline, walk quietly past a sign saying "Orphanage of Jualape." The first one moves to stand guard at the center of the porch. The second one with the petrol quietly opens the screen door and lets himself in.

Inside the Muertemos finds the room filled with beds, sixteen on each side of the long walls, all of them occupied. The children are covered with sheets. Four ceiling fans are slowly turning. He starts to pour gasoline along the floor when he sees one of the older children stirring in his bed. He tip toes over to it as he takes out a machete. When he's next to the bed he lifts up the weapon when all of a sudden we hear a whole group of children cry out. Suddenly a machine gun riddles the bedroom, as the children's cries reach a crescendo, and then there's only silence.

Back at Rodriguez's jeep, Manuel looks over to see Rodriguez, still holding his night vision binoculars, turn away in shame.

Outside the orphanage, the other Muertemos standing guard on the porch looks inside, as a look of horror comes to his face. Inside the Second Muertemos is lying dead on the floor, riddled with bullets. The children that fell out of their beds are seen to be only mannequins. "There's no children inside!" the puzzled Muertemos mutters.

"Isn't it wonderful!? " Dr. Aramos replies. Aramos grabs him from behind and throws him down to the porch floor like a rag doll.

Rodriguez again is looking through his night vision binoculars, as he sees four of his Muertemos walk into the village square. They each go to the front door of four different homes. They proceed to kick in the doors one after the other and run into the homes. The cries of men, women and children are mixed together as gunshots pierce the night.

Inside the first home the Muertemos is surprised that the home is abandoned. The Muertemos looks in disbelief as he sees the cassette recorder on a table playing. The sound of gunshot from it made him unconsciously duck for cover. He briefly smiles to himself, till he finally notices Victor looking straight at him. Victor shoots him in the throat with a cross bow.

A look of satisfaction is seen on Rodriguez's face, as he hears more gun shots in the distance. He uses his night vision binoculars to see near Jualape's Church. His smile quickly disappears when he sees one of his Muertemos fall to the ground.

From the church's bell tower, Cohen fires his sniper rifle at another Muertemos, shooting him through the heart.

Rodriguez's anger mounts as he sees through his night vision binoculars one of the four Muertemos staggering back out of a house next to the village square, an arrow lodged in his chest. It finally dawns on him that something is very wrong.

Rodriguez then looks back towards the orphanage. On the porch there, he sees a Muertemos being bitten on his neck and drained by what appears to be a vampire. The "vampire" is viciously sucking away when he suddenly stops and looks straight up at Rodriguez and smiles. Rodriguez can read Aramos's blood-stained lips: "You're next!"

"Oh shit! Oh my God! Manuel, you wear this and stay right here." as Rodriguez quickly removes his shirt and hat. Manuel, his driver, puts them on. Rodriguez climbs onto a nearby motorcycle and kicks it to life. He speeds away into the adjacent jungle.

From his vantage point of the bell tower, Cohen sees a transport truck parking in the village market. A Muertemos gets out of the back, carrying a flame thrower. While Cohen continues looking in this direction, he doesn't notice a Muertemos climbing over the edge of the ravine near the Church. On his back is slung a bazooka. Once he climbs over, he gets down on one knee as he loads a rocket into the back of it.

As Dr. Aramos passes by a nearby barn, he can see the Muertemos with the bazooka. Following where it's pointed, he can see that Cohen is the target in the Church Bell Tower. Aramos quickly grabs a knife from a killed Muertemos nearby and flings its side handed in one smooth motion towards the Muertemos. The knife slashes through the air in a straight path and strikes the Muertemos through his helmet and into his forehead. A look of bewilderment is seen on his face before he falls back into the ravine. Before he goes over the edge, he fires the bazooka into the ravine at a 45 degree angle.

Cohen is shocked as he hears the bazooka and sees the Muertemos falling over the ravine's edge. When he points his rifle back towards the opposite direction and looks through the scope as he pans across, he sees Aramos near the barn, smiling at him and giving him the thumbs up.

Cohen smiles to himself.

In the same ravine clearing he used yesterday, Henry gets a strange look on his face as he hears the whistling of the bazooka rocket. It impacts and explodes only five yards away from the front of his helicopter. "Jesus!" Henry shouts.

From the bell tower, Cohen scans the market place again and lines up the Muertemos with the flame thrower in his cross hairs. He fires his rifle and hits him in the chest. The Muertemos is knocked over onto his back. He fires the flame thrower at the back of the transport truck. The canvass covering the back of the truck is engulfed in flames, as are the two Muertemos who were hiding in the truck and now jumping out of it. They fall to the ground, writhing in pain.

One of Cohen's men passes by the orphanage and is shocked to see the pale, dead Muertemos lying on the porch, the wounds of his neck gaping wide. Cohen had warned his men that they may encounter such victims, but even battle-hardened men never get used to all atrocities.

Victor suddenly comes to the top of the hill overlooking Jualape's Center, Cohen right behind him. Manuel sees them and quickly puts the jeep in reverse. Victor runs and jumps onto the hood and then shoots Manuel in the arm. He rolls off the hood as the jeep continues going back till it hits a tree. Victor reaches the jeep first, followed by Cohen. "Les, Rodriguez is gone! He must have left this fat piece of shit as a decoy."

"Oh my God.", as Cohen grabs his walkie talkie. "Henry! Henry!?"

"Yes sir." Henry crackles back.

"Come pick us up on the double, village square. And radio Paul to be on the look out for Rodriguez."

"Yes sir, I'm on my way." Henry flips switches to fire up the Huey's engine, as the rotors kick into life.

Back on the hill overlooking Jualape's Center, Victor points his pistol at the fat Muertemos masquerading as Rodriguez.

"Where did Rodriguez go?" Victor demands.

"By now, he should be fucking Cohen's sweet puta......" Before he has a chance to finish, Cohen shoots him in the head.

"Let's go!" Cohen and Victor run to the village square, as Henry swoops down to land. Cohen goes in the copilot's door, while Victor jumps into the side entrance. As the Huey starts to lift off, Aramos is seen running to it from behind, and before it speeds away, he grabs onto one of the landing gear and hangs on as it heads for Cohen's home. Victor sits at the edge of the side door, a submachine gun in his hands, as he scans the ground below in hopes of getting a clear shot of Rodriguez.

As the Huey rushes over the rain forest's canopy, Aramos' feet are brushing against the top of the trees, forcing him to swing his legs up to rest on the landing gear as well. Above, Victor wonders if he's imagining that something's hanging on below…

Moments later, the Huey approaches Cohen's home from behind, and as it starts to pass over its roof, Aramos jumps off and onto it. The Huey continues to fly over the home before landing in the front. Cohen and Victor run out, when they see Paul lying in a pool of blood near the front door, apparently shot in the back. They split up, Cohen going through the front entrance while Victor heads to the back.

Cohen silently climbs the curved stairway, his pistol in his right hand. He walks catlike down the hallway as he nears his bedroom. He peers in from the edge before entering, keeping his right arm extended as he sweeps the pistol from left to right.
He sees the bathroom door is open. He enters it and turns on the light.
On the floor he finds Ariana's brush. He quickly leaves the bedroom and heads towards the library. He observes light under the door. He quietly pushes down the door handle and pushes the door open.

"Come in Cohen. Join us".

Cohen walks in to see Rodriguez holding Ariana next to his right, holding a pistol to her head. They're standing in the center of a beautifully laden library. Ariana is dressed in a short night dress, her orange panties seen through the nearly transparent negligee.

"You betrayed me you cock sucking Jew! Drop your gun, or I'll blow her head away right now."

"There's no need to hurt Ariana, keep her out of this." He drops his pistol to the floor.

"Kick it over here." Cohen does as he asks. As Rodriguez focuses on the sliding gun, Cohen quickly reaches for a Ninja star hidden in a padded inside pocket at the back of his pants, then palms it as he brings his right hand to his side. Rodriguez picks the pistol off the floor and puts it in his left front pants pocket.

"After I kill you, I'm going to fuck your woman till she's raw, then make her a putana for a Muertemos' whore house." Without warning, Aramos crashes through the library's skylight, as Rodriguez looks up in disbelief and horror. Aramos lands squarely on his shoulders, sprawling him forward onto the ground. Rodriguez's pistol is knocked out of his hand, Cohen grabbing it immediately. Aramos proceeds to kick Rodriguez in the groin from behind, causing him to turn on his back, writhing in pain. Aramos pulls out Cohen's pistol from Rodriguez's front pants pocket, and tosses it to Cohen. Aramos gently takes Ariana by the arm, moving her away from Rodriguez, motioning her to join Cohen.

"Les, take her to safety. I have some unfinished business with Rodriguez."

Before Cohen can act, Rodriguez stands up and stabs Aramos in the back with a switchblade he had hid in his right boot. Aramos briefly cries out, as his fangs are seen. He quickly turns around as Rodriguez holds up his small crucifix on his neck to face him. Aramos pulls it off his neck and kisses it lovingly. He then strikes Rodriguez down to the ground, pulling the knife out of his back with his right hand. He grabs Rodriguez by the groin with his left hand, lifting him halfway off the ground, Rodriguez's shoulders and bent head are against the floor.

"You won't be needing these anymore." Rodriguez screams out, as Aramos cuts Rodriguez's testicles off, his body blocking our view. Cohen covers Ariana's eyes, and Cohen himself looks away from the viciousness of Aramos's attack. Aramos drops the knife to the floor. Rodriguez turns to face Cohen and Ariana.

Rodriguez pleads through his pain: "Help me...." Cohen lowers his eyes. Aramos picks Rodriguez up by his hair with his right hand, as he plunges his teeth into his neck, again the view is obscured by Aramos's head and body. Rodriguez's body jerks up and down, as Aramos feeds greedily. When he finishes, he drops Rodriguez's limp body to the floor. He wipes his mouth off with his shirt sleeve. Aramos slowly turns back to Cohen and Ariana. His fangs slowly disappear, as a calm comes to his face.

Victor comes into the library now. A look of shock comes to him as he sees Rodriguez on the floor. Victor quickly moves next to Cohen and Ariana. Ariana looks away from Aramos, hiding her head against Cohen's chest like a little girl. A look of great sadness comes to Aramos's face, as he looks pleadingly towards Ariana. She continues to bury her face in Cohen's chest. Cohen sees this and is saddened himself.

"I'm sorry to have disappointed you Ariana. Have a good life together." Aramos starts to leave, walking sadly towards the library door, with his eyes down. Cohen puts his hand gently on Hector's shoulder to stop him.

'Don't go Hector. Ariana, you should be ashamed of yourself. Hector just saved both of our lives. Why should you fear him? He is a good man. He had the same supernatural powers when he had dinner with us. When I spoke with him alone, and when you spoke with him you saw his true humanity, his kindness, how he opened up to you about the loss of his daughter, a tragedy we can only imagine about. What has changed in him? He's a true friend, who you just broke his heart. We all owe this man a debt of gratitude that will take a lifetime to pay back. We should all approach him with love and embrace him for what he has done." Ariana looks towards Hector with tears in her eyes. "Victor, you go first!"

They all crack up at this. Ariana walks over and embraces Aramos warmly. "Forgive me Hector. I don't understand why you can do what you did to Rodriguez. God knows he deserved it, and I know you deserved my faith in you. Can you ever forgive me?"

"Of course I will!"

"Are you alright?" Aramos is moved by the look of concern and tears in her eyes.

"Yes my child, I'm fine, see?" Aramos turns to show her his back, as he lifts up his shirt to find the stab wound has nearly healed.

"How are you Ariana? Did he hurt you?"

"No, he wanted to wait till Les came home."

"Les, you really knew about how I had changed?"

"Yes Hector. I already knew you were more than you pretended to be, the night you had dinner with us, that's why I killed the Muertemos before he could shoot you in Jualape. I didn't want your cover to be blown. And besides, I still needed your medical skills if I were wrong!"

"Are those the only reasons?"

"No, Ariana would never forgive me if you should ever get hurt." Both men smiled at this.

"But how did you know?"

"When Victor here was fitting your peristaltic pump with a battery pack, he discovered that its fuse was blown, which must have happened when lightning hit the interrogation center. You obviously couldn't have used it on your "patients", so I had to conclude that Father Lupe actually took me serious about the Devil's lackey ploy."

"Actually, I'm nothing of the sort, but I don't think it's a good idea to explain. I will say that I will be around to prevent any opposition to my Brother's take over."

"Of that I am sure. I believe my men and I should be able to handle the transition for now though."

"Of that I am sure as well. Thank you for what you and your men did at Jualape.

"No need to, Hector." Cohen pauses, "I have something for you." The four of them go into Cohen's office. Cohen pulls out an envelope from his top drawer.

"Rodriguez received this today from the Brazilian Embassy." Cohen hands it to Aramos, whose eyes brighten when he sees the message.

"Thank you Les so much! I need to treat a "patient" in Sao Paulo ASAP."

"Don't forget the anesthetic!" Cohen retorts.

Aramos cracks up laughing with that, as he leaves the room with the envelope in his hand.

Chapter 8

Presidential Office-5:00 AM, January 27th, 1979

The General looks haggard, as he nervously looks at his wristwatch. He sees that it's already 5:00 AM. His ash tray is overflowing with cigarette butts. The General walks over to his bookcase. From a thin drawer between two adjacent shelves he removes a pistol case.

"Something's wrong, very wrong.", The General mutters to himself.

The General brings the pistol case to his desk and opens it, revealing a Remington .45 pistol. He removes it hastily, checking to see if the chambers are filled. He suddenly hears someone approaching his office door, as he points his gun towards it. There's knocking at the door, as The General starts to shake. Almost whispering, "Who is it?"

"It's me General." Cohen replies.

"Cohen? Cohen, come right in."

Cohen opens the door and walks in, with Rodriguez's dead body slung over his shoulder, and a raincoat covering his backside. The General smiles. He stops pointing his gun.

"Cohen my boy, you succeeded!"

"Not quite General." Cohen walks to the room's center, then rolls Rodriguez's body onto the floor. The General can now see the fang marks on Rodriguez's neck, the whiteness of his skin, and the blood surrounding his groin on his pants. The General turns away to vomit.

"I didn't succeed sir. Something got to Rodriguez before I could, and his men ran away from Jualape in fear. Jualape has not been burned sir."

"Then why did you come?"

"To warn you, to show you what our fate will be like. I'm going home to Ariana to say goodbye to her. I'd suggest you should go to your family as well while there's still time. Goodbye General." Cohen walks out the door and closes it behind him. From just outside his door, The General begins to hear something he didn't think was possible, fear in Cohen's voice

"Oh no, stay away from me." Fighting is heard outside The General's office, as Cohen cries out in pain, as he's thrown against the wall. More struggling is heard, when all of a sudden he's silent, as the snap of his neck is heard. Suddenly, a sinister laughter is heard outside the door, as The General sees the door handle starting to move. As the door starts to open, a gunshot rings out. The General falls to the floor, blood pouring out of his head, his pistol next to his body. Cohen is looking in from the now open door, a brief smile passing over his face before he leaves. The General's body lies next to Rodriguez's.

Northern Jungle-5:56 AM, January 27th, 1979

It is sunrise, as the gentle rays of sunlight filter through the forest. We see Father Lupe blinking his eyes as he leaves the exit of the Mayan Temple. He is leading the people of Jualape out of the entrance of the Mayan Temple. A long line of men, women and children are filing out. A look of relief mixed with apprehension is on their faces.

"Don't worry, the Lord has provided for our safety. Come, let's go home!" Father Lupe exclaims.

Chapter 9

Sao Paulo, Brazil-9:23 PM, January 27th, 1979

In a suburb of Sao Paulo, the outside of a modest house is seen, from which one hears a Wagner opera. The neighborhood is quiet and peaceful.

Inside this home, a man in his sixties, with short cropped hair and a mustache is seen sleeping at his desk in his study, as the record finishes. The sound of the record player's needle clicking and scratching is heard as his office door starts to open.

"Herr Mengele, Dr. Mengele?" Dr. Aramos asks.

"Who the hell are you?" as he reaches for a pistol in his desk.

"Forgive me for intruding, but your front door was unlocked. I'm a representative of Colonel Rodriguez from San Mateo." Aramos waits respectfully in the doorway. A look of recognition is slowly seen on Mengele's face, as he nods.

"Ah, yes, now I recall. You want my help to get rid of your Mestizos."

"Yes, that is correct doctor."

"What's that in your hands?" as Mengele points to a large, flat package in Aramos's hands.

"I have a small gift of affection from my country, as a small token of the esteem with which you are held there. May I?"

"Please, you can unwrap it for me." as Mengele places his pistol on his desk. As Aramos unwraps it, Mengele's eyes light up.

"One of my notebooks!" Mengele gushes with delight. "How did you get it?"

"A great admirer of yours had found it in the collection of a Middle Eastern business man. He had purchased it and then donated it to us when he learned that we were to meet."

"May I see it?"

"But of course!" Dr. Aramos walks over to Mengele and hands it to him very carefully. As Mengele starts to leaf through it, gazing lovingly at it, Aramos calmly walks behind him to join in his perusal. As various pages are being glanced at, one can see blood stains on all of them, as the screams and cries of women and children are heard in the background as he turns the pages to different parts of the large manuscript.

"I was very struck by your entry on page 91".

"Oh really? Let's take a look at it together my good man." Mengele carefully searches for the entry and then lays out the book flat on the desk for both of them to see better.

"Let's see....August 2nd, 1944. After collecting 52 sets of twins, ran third attempt to change eye color through injection of ca. 0.5 cc of teal dye 941 into their eyes"... Mengele has a flashback...

Medical Block, Auschwitz, August 2nd, 1944

A young Mengele is holding down the head of a five year old boy. Mengele's face is filled with rage and madness. He plunges a syringe needle into the boy's right eye, followed by the child's heart wrenching screams of pain...

Mengele's Home, Sao Paulo, Brazil-9:26 PM, January 27th, 1979

Mengele continues to read from his lab notebook: "August 3rd, 1944. Again, an abysmal failure. More than two-thirds of the specimens contracted ocular infections. Twenty two of them are already blind. Ordered Langbein to have all 52 sets of twins sent to the gas chamber."

"Yes, Langbein!" Aramos exclaims.

"What about Langbein?", as a puzzled look comes to Mengele's face.

"He was the one who saved a Jew from this very experiment."

"What is his name, this Jew?"

"Avenidas, Judah Avenidas. He's the head rabbi in the city of Implenza. His pathetic deposition claims that you had blinded his twin brother Saul, but in your haste, you had only injected him in his left eye." Aramos pauses for a moment, holding back the urge to just snap Mengele's neck. "Perhaps you were using him as a sort of control in your experiment?"

"That is possible. But tell me, what does this Jew have to do with me?"

"He's after you. If we could bring him to you, what would you do to him first?"

"Blind him in his other eye of course!" Mengele replies with no hesitation.

"Anyway, he goes on to say that you murdered his brother and the fifty one other pairs of children that day alone, due to the failure of one of your many worthless experiments." Mengele is starting to turn red with rage. "Langbein hid him till the camp was liberated in January of '45."

Mengele can not contain his anger anymore and slams his hand on his desk. "So what does this Jew Avenidas want?"

"He wants me to punish you." Before Mengele can reach his gun, Aramos places his palms on Mengele's temples, taking care not to crush his carotid arteries, pressing only enough to cut the flow of blood temporarily, as Mengele's eyes roll back as he faints.

Some ten minutes later, as Mengele comes to, one sees that his arms and legs are tied down to the heavy, ornate desk he was previously sitting behind. This desk is now in the middle of the office. Mengele can see that the windows are blinded, and sealed with pillows and duct tape. A Wagner opera is again playing on the nearby record player.

"Today's January 27th Herr Mengele. Do you recall what important event occurred today 34 years ago." Mengele can't answer, due to his fear. He simply shakes his head, whereupon he notices all of the surgical instruments lined up on an adjacent coffee table to his right, as well as the IV line fed into his right arm. "What, cat's got your tongue? On that day, the Russian army had liberated Auschwitz. I'm not surprised you wouldn't recall that, since you were long gone before they arrived. I presume you were concerned that Stalin wanted to execute all major war criminals right away, without wasting time for any trials. Perhaps you should have stayed for that, since I'm about to give you just a taste of what Hell has in store for you. Here's to the memory of the million and a half children you helped to murder."

Aramos starts to hold Mengele's right eye open with his right hand's thumb and index finger. Mengele struggles in vain to move his head away.

From Mengele's point of view one sees that Aramos is holding a very large syringe with blue dye in it, a drop of it is seen at the end of its very long needle.

"Please feel free to scream!" Aramos suggests.

We see the record player now, as one hears Wagner's Ride of the Valkyries being pierced by Mengele's screams......

The End

Made in the USA
San Bernardino, CA
22 January 2014